KV-374-617

Acknowledgements

I am greatly indebted to Robert Taylor, Editor of the *Black Country Bugle*, for editing and serialising these stories in his weekly paper.

Also to the staff of Coseley, Dudley, and William Salt Stafford libraries for their help in getting at the facts.

And to the Friends of Dudley Castle for providing a wealth of material: details of medieval life freely given by members of the Friends sub-group, 'The Guild of the Blessed Saint Edmund' during re-enactment sessions at Dudley Castle. Also for articles by John Hemingway and others that were published in their journal *Ramparts*.

Overdue thanks to my wife Janet for her encouragement and forbearance.

And of course, to David Green for providing his wonderful illustrations, and my photographer David Hubble.

ABOUT THE AUTHOR

Born in Oxford to Black Country parents, the author returned to his roots when his mother died early and his father waltzed off in search of pastures new.

Like the main protagonist of this story, he was then raised by his maternal grandmother. He had to leave school at the age of fifteen with no qualifications, an abhorrence of learning, and the conviction that he was stupid.

By an amazing stroke of luck, he found himself working in an engineering drawing office. Here, his peers were all attending night school as part of their apprenticeship training. Night School was a fresh start, for the subjects being studied were relevant to his need to earn a wage. On completion of his HNC, he was awarded the 'Student of the Year' at Dudley Technical College. The prize awarded was a term at Cambridge University, an experience which widened his horizons further to include the study of Biblical and literary criticism.

After gaining experience at two further engineering companies (at one of which he met our artist David Green) he began work as a Research Engineer at the University of Birmingham. This great institution encourages its staff to undergo research work for the purpose of attaining degree status. A Bachelor of Arts degree was followed by a Master of Philosophy . . . both obtained by writing and submitting theses in Computer Programming and Machine Tool Technology. Not bad for an eleven-plus reject, eh?

Feeling the need to continue writing after his premature retirement, he had a fistful of poems and short stories put out in the local press and radio. And once he had submitted the first of Jacob's stories to 'The Black Country Bugle' he was riding a roller-coaster that couldn't be stopped.

Jack O' Beans

A Medieval Saga of Dudley Castle
and its surroundings

ROBERT ASTON

Published by New Generation Publishing in 2016

Copyright © Robert A.E. Aston 2016

ISBN13: 978-1-78719-112-9

www.newgeneration-publishing.com

This work of fiction is set against the background of events
which occurred in fourteenth century England.

Drawings by David Green and the author.
Cover design by Jacqueline Abromeit

 New Generation Publishing

Contents

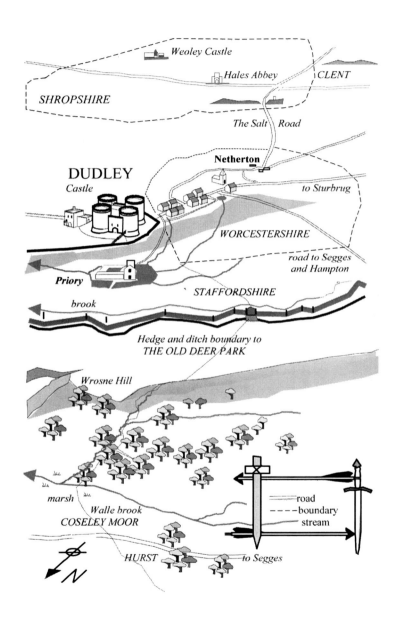

Foreword

This story is set in and around Dudley, a town in the English midlands. Towering over the town is the medieval castle, whose earthworks consist of a high conical mound with an adjoining flat area, all surrounded by a moat.

The original Norman castle would have been constructed of wood, but successive generations of barons have been replacing the timber with masonry. At the time of this story, John de Somery has just completed the reconstruction of the great Donjon or Keep.

Coal, limestone and iron ore are being mined in the surrounding area. However, it will be another five hundred years before Newcomen's 'Atmospheric Engine' allows the seams to be exploited fully. This cradle of the industrial Revolution will then become known as the 'Black Country'.

The 14th century was also a time of great change. Fortifications, weaponry and armour were evolving rapidly. The use of French by the ruling classes had begun to give way to what is now known as 'Middle English'.

The term 'Middle English' seems highly appropriate to this area, for in spite of a continuing influx of workers, the local dialect has proved to be very resistant to change. Thus, while the rest of the country has replaced the Anglo-Saxon word 'eow' with 'you', it has continued to be pronounced locally as 'yow'. Another archaism is the continued use of 'o' where modern English has adopted 'a', and vice-versa. Hence the word 'wash' is still being pronounced as it is spelt.

Such dialect words are clearly audible above the clamour of the industrial workshop. They would have had the same advantage in the clamour of the medieval battlefield.

To return to the period in hand – King Edward I is on the throne. His armies have defeated the Welsh, and he is in the process of ringing Snowdonia about with strong castles.

However, his attempts at hammering the Scots into submission are proving difficult.

Robert Aston 2009

Glossary

Arr	Yes
Aventail	A collar of chain mail to protect the throat.
Ay	Ain't
Baxter	Female baker
Bin	Are
Butt-ery	Wine store
Canstow	Can you
Cookney	Cook's assistant
Cor/cort	Can't
Cott	Small cottage
Day	Didn't
Didstow	Did you
doh/dow	Don't
Donjon	Modern 'Keep', the inner stronghold of a castle.
Dostow	Do you
Gittern	Ancient type of guitar
Glede	A live coal or ember
Hauberk	Full length coat of mail
Jed	Dead
Limner	Hunting dog
Maile	Chain mail
Neeps	Turnips
Palfrey	Docile horse used especially by women
Palisade	Fenced enclosure for defence
Psaltery	Ancient stringed musical instrument
Quiescent	Inactive
Sooth	Truth
Van	Forefront
Woh	Won't
Whum	Home
Windlass	Winch

Part One

For

four

Silver

Pennies

CHAPTER ONE

"Jacob – stop playing soldiers will yer, and come over here."

The boy paused – his wooden sword raised above his head in readiness for a downward slash at an invisible enemy.

"*Gran*! I've told yow before: it's *Jacques,* not Jacob."

From the doorway of her cottage, his grandmother smiled indulgently at his preference for the French version of his name.

"Well, who*ever* yow bin, it is time to take these pies up to market." She held out a large wicker basket, and tutted at the flour that it had left on her hessian smock.

The lad slid his sword back into his makeshift scabbard and struck what he believed to be a manly pose.

"What's it worth, then?"

"A clip around the ear-hole if yow doh. And don't think as I woh."

Jacob kicked at a pebble with his bare foot, and stared towards the distant skyline.

"But it's such a long way up to Dudley Overtun," he groaned.

"Well *I'm* too busy to go," snapped his grandmother, "and these pies won't wait." When the lad made no sign of making a move, she grew fidgety. "Your uncle James is waiting at the gate, and he's in a tearing hurry." She rubbed her hands together and tiny pellets of dough cascaded down to her eager hens. "The other baskets are already loaded on the cart and James has agreed to drop them off at the pie-stall."

The lad's frown betrayed his complete lack of enthusiasm. "Bin they for the same pie-mon as before, then?"

"Arr," said his grandmother. "The one next to the stocks."

The lad slouched over and resentfully took hold of the basket. Slumping under its weight, he sniffed the sweet aroma.

"I'm hungry," he declared.

"By all the Saints – I nearly forgot!" His Gran shooed off the chickens and vanished into the dark interior of her cottage. She emerged a few moments later, carrying a knapsack which was evidently made from the same material as her dress. Bending to place the strap over her grandson's head, she murmured: "There's a tart in here for yow and James to eat on the way. It's your favourite, Opple and Blockberry, so don't go touching none o' th' others. There's a hundred all together, and we should get at least four silver pennies for 'em." As her expression relaxed, an unbiased observer might have noted that her face had once been beautiful – before worry and hunger had taken their toll. "And as for *what's-in-it-for-yow*," she added, "if they've got any of them 'obby-'osses for sale, yow can get one fer yerself."

Jacob winced as his grandmother dug her bony fingers into his shoulder and impelled him along the path towards the front of her cottage. "But don't get payin' no more than a ha'penny for it. Them pies took a lot of working. Yow should know, Jacob. Yow collected the blockberries yourself."

"It's Jacques!" corrected the lad.

"Well... *Zyak,* stay close to your uncle... do as he says... and be sure to come straight back whum. By the way... did I mention that he's taking a cartload of beer-barrels up to the castle? After delivering the ale, he'll bring yer straight back to Netherton. Yow should be back here before dusk."

But she was talking to herself. Her grandson had already vanished around the corner of the cottage.

After handing the basket and knapsack up to his uncle, Jacob clambered up beside him on the large, four-wheeled wagon. "Good marzen, Uncle James," he said as politely as he could manage.

His uncle – a large ragged man with a nose like an over-ripe strawberry did not answer. Jacob had travelled with him before and had driven him up the wall before. Staring fixedly to the front, he released the hand brake and shook the reins. "Gee up, Blossom," he bawled as the horse lurched forward, dragging the heavily laden cart out onto the lane.

What with the rumbling of cart wheels, the creaking of barrels, and the thudding of hooves – neither of them heard Jacob's grandmother calling from her gate:

"Dow accept less than four pennies." Wrinkled lips compressed themselves into a tight little line below eyes that were clouded with worry. After all, it was going to be a very long day for the poor little mite. But at least he wouldn't go hungry. With his mother dead and his father away fighting, the lad had become unruly and headstrong. Thank the lord James had agreed to take him off her hands for the day.

Craning her neck, she screeched after the retreating cart: "And no giving your Uncle James none of your lip, neither." The last thing she needed was more strife in the family. The furrows in her forehead deepened. Why that sudden burst of enthusiasm? Her grandson had never gone off on *any* errand as willingly as *that* before. But as she opened her front door, she laughed out loud. James had never had to go to *The Castle* before.

*

"Uncle James," cried Jacob, "Can't yer make this horse go any faster?"

"No I cor," snapped his uncle. "Yow try pullin' this heavy load and see how *yow* like it."

"Can I ride on her back, then?" Jacob asked, kicking his heels together in anticipation.

"No yow cor. But I'll tell you what…" James turned to point his whip at the centre-most barrel which stood high above the others on the cart. "Yow c'n ride on *that* for a bit if y' like. It's well tied down, so yow should be safe enough." And be out of my hair an' all, he thought.

So, sitting astride his barrel and pointing the way ahead with his little wooden sword, Jacob rode his ungainly chariot.

"To the castle," he cried – over… and over… and over again.

*

"You'm going the wrong way," proclaimed Jacob as his uncle reined Blossom over to her left. Leaving the Dudley road behind, they began to skirt a large field which was divided up into narrow strips of cultivation.

"So yow knowen that, dun yer?" growled James, urging Blossom up the steepening slope. However, he had to admit that the lad was right about this not being his normal route to the town.

"This is Market Day," he said, relenting somewhat of his hostility. "The usual way in will be blocked. Anyway, the Sturbrug Road will not be so hard for Blossom to climb."

After skirting two more fields, they arrived at the main route into Dudley. But instead of immediately joining the townward procession of carts and wagons, James halted at the side of the road. Heaving back the hand-brake lever, he secured it with a clove hitch. "It's time to get off and walk," he announced.

"Why?" cried Jacob bitterly.

"Because!" said James.

"Because what?"

"Because this hill is so steep."

Actually, *all* the roads up into Dudley are too steep, he thought as he untied a rope at the right-hand side of the cart.

"And I need yer ter keep an eye on this," he added while loosening a second knot. He stepped smartly to one side as a long wooden roller dropped heavily to the ground. After dragging this round to the back of the cart, James attached it thereto with two lengths of chain so that it lay a short distance behind the rear wheels and parallel to their axle. "Use this," he ordered as he unhooked a pole from the other side of the cart. "Dow just sit there. You wants to get to the castle, dow yer?"

Reluctantly Jacob scrambled down from his perch and, slightly less reluctantly, accepted the pole. With a combined iron spike and hook at its end, it reminded him of the slashing implements that the hedge-layers sometimes used. It also made a fine spear, just like those carried by the soldiers from the castle.

Gripping the blunt end with both hands, he stepped forward to meet an imaginary enemy.

"Take that," he cried, swinging his would-be weapon around so that its vicious-looking head skimmed the ground. Unfortunately, that head was so heavy that he couldn't stop it. Spinning him around, the pole slammed itself into the forelegs of a horse that happened to be approaching from behind. Neighing its displeasure, the terrified animal tore the reins from the unprepared hands of its escort and bolted down across the field – flinging its cargo of vegetables in all directions as it careered over the strips.

"Yow young varlet!" screamed the cart-owner as his vehicle overturned and toppled the animal onto its side. "Yow'm a-gooin' ter pay fer this."

"Wass gooin' on," bellowed James, coming round to see what all the commotion was about.

"Is this your lad?" cried the farmer, trying unsuccessfully to grab Jacob by the collar.

"No it ay," blustered James. "I was just givin' him a ride on me cart."

"What was he dooin' with that then?" pointing to the pole which lay discarded on the ground.

"He must have fun it," mumbled James, shielding his eyes against the glare of the sun to stare after the capsized cart. The horse had somehow freed itself and was now drinking placidly from a stream that bisected the field. "It looks like there's no great damage done," he said hopefully. "Once we get it righted, Ja... this lad here an' me'll help yer to load her up again."

So to the accompaniment of incessant grumbling from the farmer, his cart was hauled back onto its wheels and the fruit and vegetables replaced. And once the horse had been installed between the shafts, the farmer drove her back up to the roadway.

"How about a sup o' that ale as yo'm a-carrying?" he said, eying the barrels in James's wagon.

"Them barrels are bound for the castle," James said quickly. "And they'm all sealed so I dare-not breach any of 'em."

"Yow'm one o' the Baron's men?" the farmer murmured, adopting a note of simulated respect. "Then think no more of it." And as he leapt up onto his cart and goaded his reluctant horse into motion, he added: "Perhaps yow might put in a good word for me with his Bailiff."

"Why, what 'ave yer done?"

"I'd rather not say," called the farmer as both he and his cart disappeared up the hill.

"Well, yow've gone an' done it this time," growled James, rounding angrily on the lad. "There'll be no castle for yow if I can find somebody to mind yer for the day. And in the mean time, keep an eye on that roller."

As James led Blossom out into the road, the roller followed close behind the cart, bouncing over the larger stones which littered the dusty surface. Jacob (with an occasional poke at it with his pole) trudged along at the rear.

With the road growing steadily steeper, Blossom slowed to a crawl and then ground to a halt.

"Be 'ware, lad," James cried as the handbrake proved unable to halt the cart's backward lurch. Yet it only went a couple of feet before its rear wheels encountered the roller – thus blocking further retreat. "Bin yer all right?" James hollered from the front of the cart.

"Arr!" muttered Jacob, shame-facedly. Immersed in his own misery, he hadn't been paying attention to the roller. If it had snagged or drifted off to one side, nothing could have stopped the cart from rolling backwards down the hill. And if that had happened…

"What did yer say?" called James angrily.

"I'm all right."

When Blossom had recovered enough to continue the climb, the cart lumbered into unsteady motion once more. And so they progressed: with short periods of painfully slow progress interspersed with longer pauses for resting. With the other carts overtaking them with monotonous regularity, Jacob grew angry and impatient. James ignored him completely as he coaxed and encouraged his more reliable helper to her more strenuous task. Fortunately, the roller was behaving itself and they reached the top of Overtun Hill without further mishap.

With Blossom wheezing fit to bust, they paused beside the Saxon church for her to get her breath back. Her worst ordeal was over, for from that point on, the road sloped down towards the town.

"Dow put the brake on, Uncle," cried Jacob as they began the descent. "We can get some speed up now."

"If I *dow* put the brake on,' snapped his uncle, "the cart will over-run the hoss, and that'll be the end of her... and of us, most like. In any case, how far do you think we'd get?"

Following the direction of his uncle's whip, Jacob lowered his gaze from the castle-capped hill on the horizon. From halfway down the road in front of them, carts were queuing – obviously awaiting their turn to enter the town – and, just as obviously, completely blocking the way forward. Jacob groaned. It was going to take ages to get there.

It *did* take ages before they got to the front of the queue. The land fell away on both sides, giving wide views of open countryside and blue distant hills. However, neither Jacob nor his uncle was interested in the scenery, for across the narrow ridge in front of them stretched a stout wooden fence. This prevented all vehicular access to the town – except via a pole-gate that looked barely wide enough to take the cart. Beside the gate stood a mansion – a magnificent structure of honey-coloured timbers and fresh thatch. The pole was in its 'down' position.

"What's this then, Uncle James?" Jacob moaned, kicking his barrel with his heels.

"It's the Toll gate," grumbled James, handing a small silver coin to the attendant. "They say it's to pay for new paving in the market place."

"That's right," said the attendant. "So yow c'n take that roller off the back right now. The Baron don't take kindly to anything that might damage his new paving slabs."

"Give us a hand with it then," James demanded of the attendant as he got down. "It's too heavy for one."

"Not me," muttered the attendant. "Heavy liftin' ay my job."

"Gerra move on." The shout had come from the cart behind. "We ay got all day."

And as the cries of dissent grew more numerous, Jacob surprised himself.

"I'll give yer an 'ond, Uncle James," he cried scrambling down. Together they managed to get the roller loaded back onto its hooks.

Immediately, the pole-gate was raised to allow them to progress along the side of the tollhouse. Regaining his high vantage-point, Jacob peered inquisitively in through an unshuttered window and gasped. The room was brightly lit. The rush-tapers on the walls were all alight... *even in broad daylight*. The people living there must have money to burn. Then he saw the boy. He was wearing a full suit of maile armour... and a helmet of brightly-polished iron. Even the sword that he was waving about looked as though it was made from iron. They must have been made especially for him.

Jacob scowled. Why couldn't *he* be living with a rich family like that instead of being dumped on his grandmother while his father went off to the wars?

"Bin yer all right, Jacob?" James was staring at him hard. "Yow was so quiet, I thought as yow'd dropped off."

Jacob said nothing, for now they were passing a small hovel whose sagging straw and rotting woodwork told of age and neglect – just like his grandmother's little two-roomed cott. And although the children who were playing outside were barefooted like him, they weren't wearing any pantaloons. Not everybody here was rich.

As they entered the market place, the scrunch of gravel gave way to the clack of paving slabs and the roadway doubled in width. Two-storied houses faced one another across the crowded street. In front of the houses, carts and wagons were parked – all fitted with awnings to proclaim their use as market-stalls – as did the cries of their owners. The cart rumbled along between the stalls, enveloped in a succession of mouth-watering aromas. Yet Jacob sat indifferently on his butt – oblivious to everything except his own sense of deprivation and the agonising slowness of the journey.

"Whoa!" By simultaneously hauling on the reins and the brake-lever, James brought his cart to a juddering halt. Blossom snorted with simultaneous indignation and relief, while Jacob held his nose – suddenly aware of the most horrible stench he'd ever come across. Nearby, a sullen-faced youth sat amidst a heap of rotting vegetables – trapped by his ankles in the heavy wooden vice that was the stocks. Neither Jacob nor his uncle could read what offence the youth had committed – and before they could ask anyone, the pie-seller was waving to them from behind his piles of trays.

"Hi, Jim. Another delivery from your mam?"

"Arr," shouted James, jumping down from the cart. "There's a hundred freshly-baked pies here. She cor come herself, so her's sent Jacob here in 'er stead."

"It's *Jacques,* not Jacob," shouted the lad before scrambling down from the wagon and wincing as he stepped on something hard and wet. Picking-up the discarded apple-core, he toyed with the idea of hurling it at the youth in the stocks. However, one look into his murderous eyes was enough to make him think again. Instead, he lobbed the intended missile towards the horse and scuttled self-consciously in his uncle's wake.

Winks passed between the two men as Jacob negotiated the sale of his grandmother's pies. As predicted, they fetched four silver pennies and James bit each of the wafer-thin coins in turn before dropping it into the little pouch which dangled from his nephew's belt.

"This handsel is good coin of the realm," he growled, "So yow be sure to take good care on it." Tugging the pouch closed, he turned back to the pie-seller who was busily covering the baskets with sheets of white linen. "I'll be off now then," he called. "I'd buy yer a drink... if I hadn't got a cartload of it to deliver."

"Alley Veet then, Jim," chucked the vendor, turning to confront his impatient customers. Jacob flushed with indignation. It was alright for grown-ups to use different forms for their names, so why shouldn't he do it as well?

Once they were back on the cart, James rounded angrily on his nephew: "If yow *ever* contradict me in public again," he snarled, "that'll be the last time yow ever comes out with me."

Jacob said nothing. Grown-ups never understood him. Or even tried to. He was only pretending to be a soldier from the castle. What was wrong with that? Wasn't he even allowed to pretend?

Urged on by James's whip, Blossom shouldered her way through the crowds. Seeing how resentfully the shoppers were giving way before her, Jacob smirked to himself. Usually, it was *them* shoving *him* out of the way. Now it was *their* turn to shift and they didn't like it one little bit. Not only that, from his position high up on the barrel, he could see right over their heads... across to the stalls on either side. And there was the farmer with the cart that had overturned... busily selling bruised fruit from the back of the pile. So his Gran was right about that after all.

Before long, the sights and sounds of the market faded away as Jacob lapsed into bored indifference. Even the toy-maker's stall went by unnoticed. But as they rounded a bend in the road, he saw the castle again. It was much closer now – gleaming white towers perched on their hill-top eyrie – an enormous golden flag streaming out against a clear blue sky. Jacob stared at it with hope and despair. Although his uncle had threatened to leave him behind, he seemed to have calmed down a bit in the meantime.

As if James had read the boy's thoughts, he jammed on the brake again – this time at the side of a noisy, overcrowded tent which smelt strongly of beer.

"Ain't yer going ter take me up to the castle then, Uncle James?"

"We shall have ter see."

"See what, Uncle James?"

"See if yow can learn to behave yerself."

"But me Gran said as yow was in a hurry."

"Arr. In a hurry to wet me whistle, so yow can stop that whining right *now*."

CHAPTER TWO

After lifting the peevish little boy down from the cart, his uncle led him into the beer-tent and sat him down at a table, right at the back and up against the mould-stained canvas wall. Through the haze, Jacob watched his uncle conferring with the alewife as she filled a long-necked jug from the barrel. Obviously, the woman was being asked to take care of *him* for the day. So he wasn't going to be taken up to the castle after all. And judging by the way that the woman had dealt with a rowdy customer, she wouldn't stand any nonsense from *him* either. Tears mingled with the beads of perspiration on his cheeks as bitter disappointment flooded over him.

The jug plonked heavily on the table. "I've been waiting for this," James gasped as he bestrode the bench and flopped himself down. Hoisting up the jug, he took a deep swig from it. "That's better," he murmured appreciatively.

"Is that woman gooin' ter look after me?" Jacob asked, dreading the answer.

"No, worse luck. Her's too busy."

"So are yer taking me up to the castle then?"

"As I said before, I shall have to see about that," said James, giving him a stare that could mean anything.

"But me Gran said as yow would take me."

"Did her now? Well perhaps I will... and perhaps I woh. It all depends on yow keeping out of trouble from now on. Meantime..." He produced a small horn mug from his knapsack and filled it with brown bubbly liquid from his jug. "Get this down yer wazzin and shut that miserable little gob of yourn."

Jacob took a sip. It tasted sour, but he managed to keep a straight face. At his side, his uncle drained the jug in one... long... swallow. "Now just yow sit here and behave yourself," he commanded, wiping his froth-covered mouth on his sleeve, "while I guz ter water me hoss."

Jacob took this to be an adult allusion to visiting the toilet. "Water yer horse, Uncle James?" he asked with feigned innocence.

"Arr. Blossom deserves a drink more than yow dun. After all, her's got ter drag them heavy barrels all the way up to there." James nodded his head in the general direction of the castle. "I dow know how steep the road will be, but it looks even worser than the road we've just come up."

Relieved at having been given the chance to redeem himself, Jacob took another sip from his mug. This time, it didn't taste so bad.

"Uncle James," he blurted out. "Why didn't you help yourself to the beer on the cart instead of buying it from *her*?" As soon as the words were out of his mouth, he regretted them. Such impertinence usually earned him a slap.

"Day yer 'ear what I told the farmer?" snapped James struggling to his feet. "Them casks are all sealed. If I so much

16

as tried to interfere with 'em, I'd most likely end up in the stocks… alongside that young tearaway back there."

After scrutinising the other occupants of the tent, he bent close to his nephew's ear. "Now promise me as yow'll sit here and keep out of trouble."

"I promise, Uncle."

"And no spaekin' ter nobody?"

"No, Uncle."

"All right then. I shall be back in two shakes of a lamb's tail and then we'll be off to the castle. Ally *Veet*."

"Who's Ally Veet, Uncle?" Jacob said excitedly.

"How the heck should *I* know," muttered James as he stomped off towards the entrance flap.

Now that he was sure of going up to the castle, Jacob leaned back against the edge of the table and spread out his legs in imitation of the other boozers. Canvas crackled as a gust of wind ballooned the tent, bringing with it a welcome change of air.

Just inside the entrance flap, two bearded men were teasing a third who was brandishing a sheaf of arrows in their faces. It emerged that the arrow-waver had just been disqualified from an archery contest and felt robbed of his rightful purse of silver coins. Jacob patted the pouch which rested against his thigh. Four silver pennies. His Gran *should* be pleased with him… for once.

*

Jacob didn't see the stranger, until a shadow fell across the table.

"How doo, young sir." The voice emanated from a pleasant, clean-shaven face which smiled at him over a voluminous crimson cloak. Atop the smile sat a black, wide-brimmed hat with a pheasant's tail-feather sticking out at the back.

"Now, you look like a man who can hold his ale," oozed the stranger. "A man who knows a good thing when he sees it."

Beneath Jacob's nose appeared a black leather bag. He sniffed at it disdainfully, for it smelt like something his Gran used to treat head colds. A second hand emerged from the cloak and undid the bag – whereupon the first hand tipped some of its contents out onto the table. They were beans. Round, white beans – but just beans.

"See these, laddie," the stranger whispered into Jacob's reluctant ear. "Thee'll not have seen anything like *these* before. Nor hath any man hereabouts." After a furtive glance around the tent, the stranger scooped the beans back into the bag.

"They'm nothing special," Jacob protested. "Me Gran's got some like that."

"Thou art wrong there, lad." The stranger was still smiling – but he had developed a disconcerting twitch in his right eyelid. "These beans are unique... grown from some that were washed up on the shore of the Great Western Sea."

"So what," protested the lad, searching in vain for his uncle. "What use will they be to me Gran?"

"I shall tell thee what use they will be," snapped the stranger, "if only thee'll shut up and listen."

The stranger seized Jacob's mug – drained it – and sat himself down. "Now where was I? Well... these beans are fast-growing. Even in a wet summer, they will yield *two* harvests. That's two harvests in one season, instead of one. Not only that, they are prolific. *Very* prolific."

"Pro... what?"

"Pro-lif-ic," repeated the stranger irritably. "Each of these beans will yield thousands more. And each of them, as many again. So even in a poor summer, this little bag can produce enough food to feed a small army. Knowest-ow what *that* means?" Observing Jacob's complete lack of interest, the stranger shuffled up closer. "Knowest-ow that the one that they call 'The Bruce' has rebelled against the king?"

Jacob shook his head.

"Well," continued the stranger. "Our Edward Longshanks sees himself as a second King Arthur. The high king of all Britain. He's already crushed the Walesh. And by executing William Wallace, he thought that he'd finally brought the Scots to heel."

The stranger picked up a stray bean and inserted it carefully into the bag. "But now that The Bruce covets the throne of Scotland for himself, the porridge is boiling over again." The stranger chuckled. "And the stink of it can be smelt even down here." Perceiving no glimmer of amusement, the stranger continued: "The Baron is, even now, on the way back from London after receiving his orders from the king. John de Somery is to raise a company of knights and archers to join the king's army in Scotland.

"Now where ye have fighting men, *there* ye have appetites. And the bigger the company, the bigger are those appetites. *That's* where these beans come in. Building all those castles in Wales has left Longshanks desperately short of money. So for this next campaign, he is making his commanders responsible for feeding their own men." The stranger snorted with indignation. "That's all very well for *him* to say when the harvests have been so disastrous. But Edward also says that he will allow no scavenging off the land since it makes enemies out of poor ordinary folks. Folks who don't give a coney-turd who's ruling the roost as long as there's enough food for themselves and their bairns." With a flash of surprisingly white teeth, the stranger's grin returned. "Folks like your grandmother, in fact."

At the mention of his Gran, Jacob got up to leave. Immediately, he felt his arm restrained lightly but firmly. "Even a lad like *you* must see that the Baron needs these beans."

"Then why don't you sell them to him *yourself?*" spluttered Jacob – surprised at his own quickness of thinking. The stranger put his hand over his lips to conceal them from prying eyes.

"Unfortunately," he whispered, "the guards won't let me anywhere near the castle. However, I have learned that you will be going up there within the hour."

"Arr," said Jacob. "My uncle's taking me... but only if I can keep my nose clean. So I should be getting off now."

"Get off, by all means," said the stranger. "But pray take these beans with thee. All I ask is... just... four silver pennies. Ye can be sure that the Baron will pay a great deal more than *that* to get his hands on them."

"I don't want yer rotten beans," spluttered Jacob. "Go away and leave me alone."

"Fair enough, young Sir... but I am *not* one that readily takes 'No' for an answer. Especially from a young whippet like *you*."

With that, the stranger rose to his feet and with one deft slice of his knife, detached Jacob's little pouch and hid it within his cloak. "And in return, I shall leave thee the merchandise." The bag thumped onto the table. "Look after it well, for all that I have told thee is the God's-honest truth.

"Those beans are worth a king's ransom to anyone with an army to feed." The stranger bent close to Jacob's ear: "Just tell them that *Merlin* sent thee." He paused as if for thought, before continuing: "However, perchance the name will not be enough. Thou wilt also need the password." The stranger murmured a four-syllable word into the lad's unwilling ear and immediately slipped away through an overlap in the canvas wall of the tent.

*

James returned to find Jacob crying into the skirts of the alewife.

"A mon come and took away all me Gran's money," the lad sobbed, turning tear-filled eyes up towards his uncle. "And all he left me was these rotten beans." Jacob held out the bag with a trembling hand. "He said they was special."

"What man?' cried James, glaring angrily round the tent and then back at the alewife. When she shrugged her ignorance, he slid his hand into the bag and drew out one of the beans. "Well, by the Saints," he muttered. "I ain't never seen nothing like *this* before in me whole life. And I thought as I'd seen the lot."

"They'm for feeding the soldiers," Jacob sobbed. "The mon said that we should sell 'em on to the Baron."

"Oh arr. An' the Baron is going to want to see *us* is he?" snapped James. "A carter and his lad?"

"The mon said as he *would* see us, Uncle. He told me what peace-word to say."

"Ar'll bet he did," muttered James, putting the bag carefully into the knapsack. "I dow know. I cor leave yer for a minute without yer gettin' into trouble." He patted his own pouch to make sure that it was still dangling from his belt. "Come on then, 'Trouble'."

As James hauled the knapsack onto his shoulder, he turned away to hide his grin. This journey was turning out to be far more interesting than he could ever have imagined.

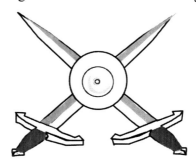

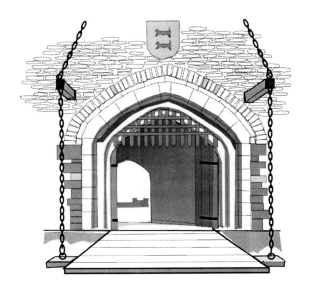

CHAPTER THREE

Jacob squirmed with excitement as the castle grew ever nearer – until a massive, wooden gatehouse barred their way. "Oh no," he squawked. "We're not stopping again."

"Just keep quiet," commanded his uncle, reaching into his pouch and producing a folded piece of parchment. Halting the cart, he held out the document to a guard who had just emerged from the gateway. His golden surcoat was emblazoned with two blue lions, just like those on the flag above the Donjon – now hidden behind high cliffs and their coronet of timber palisade. The guard's polished steel helmet was equipped with a visor and an aventail of maile.

"Is that your work?" James whispered, noticing his nephew's interest in the collar.

The area around Netherton was famous for producing fine chain-maile. And for the very best work, the blacksmiths enlisted the help of the local children – their little fingers and sharp vision being required for inserting and upsetting the tiny rivets which held the rings closed.

Having done many such stints at the forge himself, Jacob had already noted that the rings of the guard's aventail were simply butted together at their closure. As a blacksmith had once told him: 'That ay much good; unriveted rings can be forced open by a spear or sword thrust.'

"That's not one o' mine," Jacob replied with a smirk.

As the guard bent forward, his visor slid down to cover his face. To peals of boyish laughter it was raised up to reveal a countenance flushed with anger and embarrassment. James scowled a warning to his nephew, while the soldier raised the document until it was level with his eyes.

"What is that, Uncle James?" whispered Jacob.

"That be the in-voys for the ale," replied his uncle. "Signed by the Baron's Chief Steward his-self."

Finally, the guard grinned. "This all seems to be in order," he announced as he nodded for the heavy gates to be unlatched. "Ye be free to pass… but thou shalt need *these*." He tossed three black woollen scarves into the cart, where they landed heavily on the footboard.

"What do we want with *them*?" queried James.

"Thou shalt find out soon enough," muttered the guard as he swung open the gate and pointed up the roadway beyond. "Carry straight on to the cliff – then turn left. Quickly now. Ally Veet."

"So *that's* who Ally Veet is," whispered Jacob.

"I think as yow'm right," murmured his uncle, shaking the reins.

The road climbed steadily upwards until it ended in a tee-junction. As the cart slewed round into the left-hand branch, the scarves slid across the footboard – leaving a trail of dark particles on the worn surface of the timber.

"Pass us up some of that powder, Jacob. It looks familiar."

Biting his tongue at his uncle's continual use of that hated name, the lad retrieved a pinch of the black granules and dropped them into his uncle's outstretched palm. James stroked the particles with his ring-finger and touched them with the tip of his tongue. "I thought so," he declared, shaking off the granules and wiping his hand on his trousers. "It's charcoal. Now what would *that* be for, I wonder?"

It was half an hour before they found out: the half an hour that it took Blossom to drag the heavy cart up to the top of the hill. While they waited to be allowed through the palisade, Jacob and his uncle stared across it with wonder. A thick layer of mist was tumbling and flowing down the slope towards them. And out of these clouds rose a high conical mound, from which the massive drum-towers of the Donjon upthrust themselves against a sky of Coventry Blue.

The Donjon had been impressive when seen from the town. It was absolutely breathtaking now, for its masonry had been lime-washed dazzling white. And high above the battlements, two blue lions writhed on their billowing golden banner.

Realising that they had been holding their breaths, Jacob and his uncle both inhaled deeply. And both choked. These mists were not the clouds of Heaven. These were the acrid fumes of Hell.

Alerted by the sound of coughing, a guard appeared at the gate. Even though he had a scarf tied tightly over his mouth, he only stayed long enough to allow them entry. But as he retreated back to his hut, he pointed across the cloud-field to a stone-built gatehouse at its far right-hand extremity. James nodded his understanding.

"Pass us up two of them scarves," he muttered, "as quick as yow can. And wrap the other 'un round that horrible gob of yourn."

"It's Jacques," came the muffled reply, but his uncle didn't hear it. He was too busy trying to urge his reluctant horse over the mist – its hesitant feet probing uncertainly for solid ground beneath.

*

As the cart drew nearer to the gatehouse, the source of the mist was revealed: two brick-built towers that had been erected on the edge of a great ditch.

"I pity them," muttered James peering down through the fog. Jacob's watering eyes followed the direction of his uncle's gaze. Down at the bottom of the moat, the indistinct figures of workmen were filling wheelbarrows with excavated limestone – apparently intended for a third, and so far quiescent, kiln.

Jacob said nothing. He was more concerned about whether there would be solid ground all the way to the gatehouse – or a sudden drop into the swirling, stinking void. But he needn't have worried. Another mufflered guard beckoned them on, and soon they heard the clatter of hooves and wheels on the unseen planks of the drawbridge.

Pausing beneath the red-stone arch that framed the entrance to the gatehouse, James loosened his scarf and risked taking a deep breath of what proved to be almost-fresh air.

"Here we go," he muttered, glancing up at the heraldic shield at the apex and shaking the reins. "Into the lion's den!"

But Jacob was too agog with wonderment to answer. After passing beneath an iron-toothed portcullis, they were now entering a dark and gloomy passage. Its ceiling curved over like the inside of a barrel, magnifying the creaks of the heavily-loaded cart and the clatter of the horse's hooves as she struggled to haul it up the flag-stoned incline.

Directly above their heads, a trapdoor opened and immediately crashed down again. Startled by the loud report, the horse lunged forward – propelling her passengers out through a second portcullised portal and into the open air. By the time James managed to haul her to a standstill, they were at least twenty yards out into the high-walled courtyard of the castle.

Jacob had been hoping to see knights in armour, riding full-tilt at one another in front of a cheering crowd. But the courtyard was silent and deserted. And even *he* could see that this was not the best place for jousting; its two acres of churned-up turf sloped down to a second but less-imposing gatehouse at the far end.

With no one there to receive them, James wheeled his cart around and drove it back up towards the gate they'd come in by. Above and to the right of this, the Donjon on its mound blocked out the noonday sun – casting a dismal shadow over everything. Just as its owner did.

"It seems that the Baron can-nay trust his own men," James observed as he drew up beside a defensive ditch which skirted the inner-side of the mound. This section of moat was completely free of fumes so they had a clear view along its short and curving length. Down at the far end (where it was blocked-off by the curtain-wall) two maile-clad knights were crouching like silver statues. Each held a sword in his right hand and what looked like a saucepan lid in the other.

Suddenly, the knight farthest away from them dashed forward along the muddy bottom of the ditch. Swinging his sword backwards and up over his head, he hacked down at his opponent's helmet. Quicker than it takes to tell, his adversary rammed his little shield against the hilt of his own sword and raised them both to turn aside the blow. Even before the echo of the clash had died away, the men had resumed their former crouching positions. Jacob gawped, unable to believe that *anybody* could have moved so fast – especially when wielding such heavy-looking swords.

Paying no heed to their uninvited audience, the combatants continued to watch each other like hungry hawks. Obviously, one of them was about to strike out, but which one would it be? Neither of them was giving any hint of his intentions by the slightest flexure of muscle or wavering of weapon.

"Hey, Carter!"

That irate shout had come from the direction of the gatehouse. An angry-looking soldier was hurrying towards the cart, his golden surcoat flapping about his polished leather kneecaps. "Come away from there," he bawled, pointing towards a row of wooden out-houses on the far side of the courtyard. "The butt-ery's over there."

After getting James to pull up beside a shed full of barrels, he held out a gloved hand.

"Let's have your in-voys," he commanded. Without even glancing at the docket, he handed it to a short pensive man who had come shuffling out of the dark interior of the butt-ery.

"Watchman," the shuffler whispered. "Dostow know if this consignment is for the gentry – or is it just 'small-ale' for the men?"

"How should *I* know?" the Watchman muttered. "Thou shouldst know that thyself." But as he and the Butt-ler studied the writing, he admitted: "There is nothing to indicate that here." Folding up the parchment, he tucked it into his pouch. "The Steward will know. I've got to go up to the Donjon, so I'll ask *him*." He glanced across at James, who was slumped in the driver's seat like a sackfull of neeps. Hurriedly retrieving the parchment from his pouch, the Watchman thrust it towards the Butt-ler once more. "Just make sure that none of that ale has gone missing."

While his uncle and the Butt-ler were busily checking the barrels, Jacob had nothing to do but gaze idly around the courtyard. Around the perimeter of that turreted and battlemented enclosure stood several wooden buildings and a few that were built of fresh-hewn limestone. But apart from his uncle, the Butt-ler and the Watchman (who was now hurrying back to the gatehouse) there was still nobody about. He couldn't see the swordsmen, although he could hear them going at it hammer-and-tongs down there in the moat.

Nevertheless, he had the uncomfortable feeling of being watched. Inevitably, his eyes were drawn back to the Donjon. Between its massive drum-towers, a pair of lancet windows were staring back at him in blank astonishment. Below them, a red-lipped archway bared its portcullis-fangs – warning him that he had no business being there.

Yes he had! He had Merlin's beans!

"I want to see the Baron," Jacob yelled to the Watchman – who was directing a cartload of bread to the next building along.

"Yow've gone and done it now," Uncle James whispered, poking him in the small of his back. "Yow and yer big gob."

The Watchman scowled, muttered something under his breath and stomped back to the cart.

"What was that?" he barked.

"I've got something for the Baron."

"Oh yeah? And what might *that* be?"

"I can only tell that to the *Baron*."

The Watchman glared across to the lad's guardian – who was pretending to pacify his horse while the barrels were rolled down a ramp at the back of the cart. "The Baron is in London," he bellowed, turning on his heel. "Come back another day."

"I cor come back," cried Jacob. "*Merlin* sent me."

"*Who* sent thee?"

"Merlin."

"So what did this… *Merlin* say… that makes it so *urgent*?"

"He told me the *peace-word*."

"Artow taking the p—?"

"No, Sir,' interrupted James hastily. "He's just a daft young lad. What he really meant was 'password'."

"I know what he meant," snapped the Watchman. "So what *is* this *peace*-word, then?"

As Jacob repeated the four-syllable word, the Watchman's smirk faded. Visibly shocked, he seized the lad's arm in an iron grip. "Keep quiet about this," he snarled, "or it will be the worse for thee."

"God knows what yow've got us into now," muttered James under his breath.

Jacob said nothing.

Summoning the two combatants up from the moat, the Watchman placed them in charge of the newcomers.

"They are not to talk to anyone," he yelled as he marched purposefully off towards the Donjon.

With eyes carefully averted, the guards stationed themselves on either side of the wagon – their maile-clad fists resting on swords almost as long as Jacob was tall. While the boy tried unsuccessfully to question the guards about their equipment, James remained plunged in thought. He had been told that this place was dangerous, and now he was about to find out for himself. As though in confirmation, a long drawn-out wail echoed around the courtyard, causing the hairs on the back of his neck to stand to attention. Some poor soul was suffering the torments of Hell. Was it going to be *their* turn next?

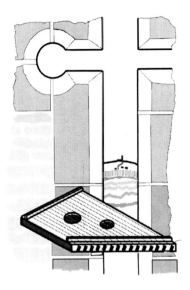

CHAPTER FOUR

On hearing three short horn-blasts from the direction of the Donjon, Jacob and his uncle were compelled to follow the Watchman around the side of the gatehouse. After crossing an enclosed drawbridge and climbing a flight of steps, they were brought to a halt in front of the great oaken doors of the Donjon itself. The blood-red stonework of the archway contrasted alarmingly with the whitewashed masonry in which it was set.

"Into the mouth of the lion," muttered James, gazing up at the spiked teeth of the portcullis. "God help us now," he added as one of the doors swung open. At his side, Jacob trembled silently.

After words had been exchanged with the guard, the pair were hurried up a narrow winding staircase – emerging giddy and apprehensive into a spacious but gloomy hall on the first floor. Tattered banners hung down from the ceiling, swaying gently in the updraught from a brazier in the middle of the hall.

Marching their charges to the centre of the room, the guards saluted, stomped their boots and retired to take up positions on either side of the door – the only visible way out.

The darkness of the chamber seemed intensified by a narrow ray of sunlight. Emerging from an arrow-slot window, it slashed down through the swirling smoke to fall across a massive oaken table. Beside the table stood the Watchman... and seated behind it was the hunched figure of a man. Although the seated man's face was hidden in shadow, he was obviously staring hard at his prisoners.

"Come over here, willtow?" the seated man commanded. "So that I can see you clearly." As the pair shuffled forward, the seated man picked up a candlestick and handed it to the Watchman. "Light it."

Without a word, the Watchman turned to the brazier behind him – ignited the candle, and placed it carefully on the table.

The seated man leaned forward. "That's better. Now at least I can see their faces."

They could also see his: a full head of jet-black hair, a well-trimmed beard to match, and a stare that could curdle milk. His unblinking eyes flickered from one to the other: "A Carter and his lad, eh?... and both strangers here. So *HOW CAME THEE TO KNOW THE PASS-WORD OF THE DAY?*" At the sudden outburst of his master, a hidden harpist stopped his plucking.

The carter bowed his head, either out of simulated respect or from genuine fear.

"A stranger told it to the lad, my Lord," he said, in words that were scarcely audible above the snarling of the hounds beneath the table. Yet even *their* growls couldn't obscure the ringing notes of the harpist who had now resumed his playing.

Apart from his home-made whistles, the only musical instruments that Jacob had ever heard were the bagpipes at the village dances. This music was different... sad and yet gaye *at the same time*.

"TELL ME, *BOY,* WHO WAS THIS STRANGER?"

Startled, the boy choked on his own spittle. As he strove to formulate an answer, his questioner continued – using a calmer tone that was nevertheless pregnant with menace: "Hadestow ever seen him before?"

Jacob's mind whirled frantically. He hadn't done anything wrong, yet he was in serious trouble.

"There was this m-man in the t-tent," he stammered. "He... he c-come up... and he s-sold me some b-beans."

"And *where* did this... commerce occur?"

"In the b-beer-tent. Down there in D-duddeley Over-t-tun." Jacob stared longingly through the arrow-slit window. Far below, the market-place lay strung out along the so-called High Street. Even from that distance he could see that the stallholders were leaving. Perhaps it was the effect of the music, but he now felt calmer, somehow detached from the proceedings.

The seated man eased himself in his chair and turned to face James.

"So, Carter. Ye left this young lad alone in that den of thieves and cut-purses?"

James hung his head and said nothing.

"And what did this... bean-seller look like?" demanded the seated man, strumming his fingers on the table.

"I do not know, for I never saw him," muttered James. "He had left before I got back."

"Knowestow the pass-word, Carter?"

"No, my Lord. I never heard it.

The seated man studied James as a cat watches a sparrow. Suddenly, he waved one of the guards across from the doorway. "Take this oaf down to collect his dues... *NO, NOT YOU, LAD*. You are to stay here with me."

Through tear-filled eyes, Jacob watched his uncle being escorted away. The seated man placed both hands on the table and heaved himself to his feet. He was a giant of a man – tall and broad-shouldered – and dressed from head to foot in black leather. The floorboards shook to the stamp of his boot. "I NEED ANSWERS AND I NEED THEM *NOW*."

"What?" cried Jacob, scared witless by the fury in his interrogator's shouting.

"What me no whats," cried the man. "I, Chief Steward to the Baron, command thee. Describe to me this stranger."

In faltering words, Jacob described the man in the tent.

"...And he told me to say as his name was *Merlin*," he ended hopefully.

"Merlin?" The name evidently had some importance.

"And he left me these beans to sell to the Baron." Jacob held out the bag.

"And why should the Baron be interested in buying beans from a mere *boy*?"

"They'm special beans. The mon said as they would feed an army."

The Steward resumed his seat, untied the bag and tipped a few of the beans onto the table. He shook his head.

"I think we can manage well enough without such meagre fare as *this*." Picking up the bag, he tossed it into the brazier – where it began to blaze with a bright blue flame.

Horror-struck, Jacob watched as thick grey smoke poured down onto the floorboards. It flowed across them – even drawn down into the cracks by the draught.

"Don't burn *my beans*," he cried as soon as he recovered his power of speech. "They cost me a lot o' money."

"INSOLENT CAITIFF!" shouted the Steward. Flushed with anger, he waved the remaining guard over from the doorway. "Take this brat down to the cells, where... he is... to... remain... there... to... remain... until... until..."

The hounds had already fallen silent as the Steward fought against the drowsiness that threatened to engulf his mind. Suddenly, Jacob remembered the scarf that was still hanging about his neck. By the time he had it tied over his mouth, the room was completely filled with evil-smelling fog.

"Hello?" he whispered fearfully. But came there no reply.

Hidden by the fumes, the Steward lay sprawled facedown across the table, with the Watchman slumped against the leg of his chair.

Jacob groped his way towards the door. Losing his way in the murk, he blundered into the unconscious figure of the minstrel – sagging in his chair with his box-shaped harp resting on his knees. Even in his desperation, Jacob couldn't resist the temptation to pick up the instrument – although whether he intended to take it with him or not, he couldn't have said. The psaltery decided the matter for him, when the sharp end of one of its wire strings pierced his finger. As the lad cried out, the instrument bounced on the hidden floorboards – sending a long, discordant chord ringing throughout the hall. Nobody stirred.

Not even the hounds. And Jacob was no longer there to hear the dying echo.

It only took a few seconds for the lad to grope his way down the spiral staircase to the doorway. But as he attempted to slip though it, a spear-staff descended to bar his way.

"Halt!" cried its owner – a tall man, chain-mailed and indignant. "Where is thy guard?"

"He's s-still up there... with the Steward, Sir."

"And they allowed thee to depart from the Donjon unaccompanied? How can this be?"

"They were busy… but they did tell me what *peace-word* to say."

"Which is?"

Jacob whispered the four-syllable word.

The guard laughed out loud: "Yow'd better *peace-off* then, lad."

Jacob needed no further urging, for he was hurtling hell-for-leather towards the drawbridge. Another declaration of the password got him out into the courtyard, where his uncle was waiting anxiously beside his cart.

"Get me out of here, Uncle," cried Jacob. "They'm all jed up there."

"What have yow done now?" shouted his uncle. "And *now* I suppose yow expecting *me* to get yer out of it." And yet James had promised to take good care of the lad. "Yow'd better jump up on the cart then," he urged. "These barrels are empty and there's one big enough for yow ter hide in."

Back on the cart, James hoisted up a huge cask and lowered its open end over his cowering nephew. Springing into the driving seat, he urged Blossom into a brisk – but not *too* hasty – trot.

*

Two days later, Jacob was playing in the yard behind his grandmother's cottage once more.

"There he is," came a shout from the other side of the hedge. "That's the lad."

Before the lad could reach the safety of the cottage, he found himself surrounded by armed soldiers. Brandishing his little wooden sword, he faced his captors – who immediately formed themselves into a ring of bright blades and faceless visors around him. One soldier, who had remained outside the circle, raised his visor.

"Artow the lad that came up to the castle?" he demanded. "The one they are calling 'Jacques o' the beans'?"

"Certes he is," cried the Steward, strolling into the yard – resplendent in shining maile and glowing surcoat.

"It weren't me, mister," protested Jacob as his grandmother emerged to see what all the fuss was about.

The Steward turned to the fearful woman. "Ah, good-wife. Artow the baker of this most excellent crusade?" On the palm of his half-extended gauntlet lay a half-eaten pie.

Jacob's grandmother took the crust and held it up close to her eyes. "Arr... this be one o' mine," she admitted. "Yow can tell by the pattern. Why dun yer want ter know, my Lord?"

"At last," cried the Steward, turning to his men. "We have found the baxter who makes pies fit for a king." He placed a maile-clad arm along the old woman's skinny shoulders and his smiling bewhiskered mouth beside her ear.

"For years, we have sought the baxter of this delicious fare," he whispered. "But the stall-holder keeps his secrets well... even from the Baron himself." Stepping back, the Steward took the old lady's wrinkled hand between his ironclad fingers.

"Well Goody... from this day forward, thou shalt reside with us at the castle. There shaltow cook pies for the whole De Somery family. And later... when the time for war is nigh – as many as may be needed to feed our army." He turned his face to his men. "But I beseech thee, mistress," he cried, "Do not make *theirs* so tasty... *or we shall never get them to fight*." He roared with laughter, while his guards guffawed ironically.

With the Steward's iron grip upon his shoulder, Jacob felt himself being guided towards the front gate of the cottage. "Well, Jacques. We shall make a swordsman of thee yet."

At a respectful distance, his grandmother followed – shaking her head in wondering disbelief.

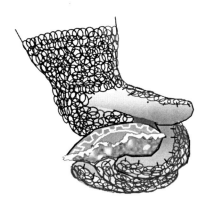

Part Two

Jacob
and the
Arrows of
Doom

CHAPTER FIVE

"So this is the *kitchen* then, is it?"

Jacob's grandmother wrinkled up her nose and gazed about the large but shabby room with unconcealed disdain. "When I saw all that fancy stonework on the way up to the castle, I was expecting something better than *this*."

Gran, her grandson Jacob, and a self-important-looking individual, were standing just inside the threshold of a large shed-like building. It was built from rough wooden planks, set upright in a floor of trampled earth. From a fire in the centre of the room, sparks rose like tiny rubies and vanished into the clouds of smoke that were swirling about in the shadowy roof-space.

The chief cook (for that is who the individual was) huffed himself up with indignation. His feathers had been well and truly ruffled… 'feathers' of bright blue velvet with golden trimmings.

"In all the Baron's lands," he crowed, "nowhere shaltow find a better kitchen than *this*. Here, we have everything thatow could require." Pointing with his iron-shod staff, he drew the old lady's attention to the comprehensive range of facilities: "*There*, are the spits for the roasts... *There*, the chains for the cauldrons... *There*, the tables for preparation... the mortars and pestles... and *there*—"

"So *where* am I supposed to bake pies, then?" interrupted Gran impatiently. "Ar cor see no ovens."

"The bake-house is next door,' snapped the Chef. "We have ovens a-plenty there."

"And is *that* made from old bits of wood an' all?" asked Gran.

"Certes it is!" protested the Chef. "All the kitchens are constructed like this." He threw up his forearms in a gesture of helplessness. "After all, the cookneys are always leaving the fires unattended and it only takes one spark for the whole lot to go up in flames." He flicked a smoking glede back into the fire with the tip of his staff.

"We have to re-build these kitchens so often that there is no point in making a very grand job of it."

"And *those* are the *cookneys*, bin 'em?" Gran cast a withering glance at two young men who were carrying a large, but empty tray from one bench to another.

She sniffed contemptuously. "Neither on 'em seems to be doing any cooking."

"Those are indeed my cookneys," confirmed the Chef. Before Gran could make any further comment, he tapped his staff against an earthenware pot which stood beside the fire. The dullness of the clank suggested that it was full of water. "A moment of your time," he cried with authority. "This *lady* here... is the Baron's new *Baxter*."

The Chef's irony was not lost on Gran. Nor on the youths. They looked up briefly, grimaced, and then resumed their examination of the tray. Neither of them had spoken or even smiled.

"They were both hoping for promotion," whispered the Chef behind his hand. "But between you and me, they wernay up to it."

Gran sniffed once more, and turned to face the official. "And what makes yow think as *I* am up to it?" she queried – hands on hips – her toothless jaw working up and down as if chewing on air.

"Oh!" cried the Chef. "We have been enjoying your pies for years... but up until now, we have had to purchase them in the market place." He lowered his voice conspiratorially. "The Baron will not allow any others past his lips."

"I have-na been charging enough for them then," muttered Gran, hoisting up her hessian skirts in imitation of the fine ladies she had seen strutting about in the courtyard outside. "Let us see your bake-house then," she demanded.

The bake-house was much the same as the kitchen: with similarly planked walls and a steeply sloping thatched roof. But instead of the central fire, three stone-built ovens stood against the opposite wall. They were dark and cold.

"Is no one doing any baking, then?" queried Gran, eyebrows raised to indicate her amazement.

"No! Our baker has been taken ill, so we are having to get our bread from the market-place as well."

Gran scrutinised the scrubbed-top wooden bench and the large wooden trough for mixing dough. "This woh do," she declared. "This is all for baking *bread*."

"I am sure that we can find a little corner for *thee*," muttered the Chef impatiently.

"That ay no good to me," snorted Gran. "I needs me own space." Start as yow mean to carry on, she thought.

"That will *not* be possible," snapped the Chef. Suddenly, he seemed to pull himself together, for he drew himself up to his full height. "Know thy place, old woman," he growled, glaring down upon her un-tressed grey hair.

"Ar knows mar place all right," replied the old woman, turning towards the door. "And it ay here."

"Wait!" cried the Chef – angry, but also relieved that no one else had witnessed the contra-pleading. "Stop *just* where you are."

Gran paused in the doorway. "Yow cort hold me here."

"That is exactly what I *can* do," retorted the Chef. "The Baron says that you are here for good... and so... whether you like it or *not*... you are here for *good*."

"Oh ar?" snorted Gran. "And whose good might *that* be? Yourn or mine?"

"Both!" said the Chef.

"And if I refuses?"

The Chef glowered past the old woman to the open door, where one of the cookneys was lurking with his ear cocked like a hearing-trumpet. After he had sent the youth packing, the Chef marched back to the old woman and seized her by the shoulders.

"We have ways of making you work," he snarled.

Up until then, Jacob had remained silent – but now, he remembered the blood-curdling scream that he had heard on his first visit to the castle.

"That is true, Gran," he cried. "They torture folks up here."

"We... torture... people?" repeated the Chef, baffled by the allegation. As far as he was aware, nobody had ever been tortured in the castle. And yet he was grateful for the lad's assertion; it might persuade the old woman to be more reasonable. After all, it was the Baron's expressed command that she should be accommodated here... and the Baron did not take kindly to being obstructed. Suddenly, the Chef bared his teeth in a grin – that his audience interpreted as a grimace of cruel anticipation. It was – but the malice was not directed against them. No! The Chef had just remembered the peacock's infernal squawking: it *did* sound like a soul in torment. With any luck, he would soon have it roasting on one of those spits next door.

"Yow cor frighten me," bluffed Gran, sticking out her chin to conceal her fear. "I am an old woman now and my life has but a little time to run. If yow kills me, it will-nay be such a great loss. At least, I shore have to toil all day just to earn enough pennies to feed us… Aye; and to feed yow lot an' all what with yower taxes and yower tolls. Anyway, a priest once told me that when I die I shall goo up to heaven. Where I shall see my beloved daughter again. And another thing—"

"Oh, for God's sake shut up," cried the Chef. As he turned away in exasperation, his gaze fell upon Jacob – who was now cowering behind his grandmother's skirts.

"But the *lad* is not old," he whispered into the old woman's ear.

"Yow would nay kill a bairn," Gran wailed. Yet she was quite sure that they would, if it suited them.

"Nay," admitted the Chef, regretfully. "But I can make his life a living hell while he is here."

"Do *that,* and I shall pyzon the lot on yer," hissed Gran.

"You would regret it."

"Not as much as *yow* would!"

Suddenly, the Chef's antagonism seemed to evaporate.

"All right," he groaned, mopping his brow with a spotless white kerchief. "Have it your own way."

"And we can have a baking-house all to ourselves?" asked Gran, increasingly aware of her strong bargaining position.

"I shall have to consult the Steward of course, but I *think* that something can be arranged." He placed an arm reassuringly around her shoulders. "And since you will need assistance, I shall arrange for one of the cookneys to help you."

"Oh no yow *woh*," protested Gran, shrugging off the arm. "Before I knows it, all me secrets will be out. All the wisdom of me mother (and me grandmother a-fore 'er) will be common knowledge."

The Chef stood silent, for that had indeed been his plan.

"So who *shall* I get to help you then?"

Gran turned to her grandson and pushed him forward.

"Jacob."

"But I nay not *want* to be a cookney," snorted Jacob, taking heart from his grandmother's incredible display of defiance. "The Steward said as I could train to be a sword-fighter."

"And WHAT is the matter with being a COOK?" bellowed the Chef. In spite of his high status, he was susceptible to any slight on his profession – even from a bare-footed young urchin like this one.

Gazing into the far distance, Gran tapped Jacob on his head.

"The Steward *did* promise that," she confirmed, keeping up the thumping in spite of the lad's increasing antagonism. "But – I – still – need – him – to be – with – *me*."

"All right. All right," spluttered the Chef. "The lad *shall* help thee. But only in the forenoon. Until... Undrentide. And after *that*, he shall help the other scullions about the castle."

"Doing what?"

"Carrying baskets of mortar for the masons... mucking-out the latrines. Things like that. Dostow agree?"

"Agreed," said Gran, smirking with satisfaction and wiping her hand on her skirt.

"*Ar* dow agree," spluttered Jacob. "I want to be a *soldier*."

46

"Indeed," murmured the Chef, thoughtfully. "Well! If you are a *very* good little boy, I shall recommend thee for... for... for retrieving the arrows at the butts."

"Now that is decided," declared Gran, interpreting Jacob's thoughtful silence as willingness. "Where dun we sleep?"

The Chef looked flustered for a moment, and then he smiled. "Why! In thine own little corner of this bake-house." He indicated the far end of the hut, where one of the ovens stood a little apart from the other two. "I shall have that end of it partitioned off for thee. After all, you would nay wish to sleep with the *cookneys*, would thee?"

"And the lad will sleep in there with me?"

"Why yes! Of course."

This was *not* good news as far as Jacob was concerned. Observing his reddening face, his grandmother stroked his hair in an ineffectual attempt at smoothing it down.

"Nay to worry, Jacob," she murmured. "Yow has *nothing* that I have-nay seen afore."

CHAPTER SIX

Early the next morning, one of the cookneys thumped loudly on the partition which now separated-off Gran's end of the bakery. "THERE IS A MEETING OUTSIDE," he yelled through the insubstantial boards. In their respective corners, Jacob and his grandmother were catapulted into consciousness – disconcerted at first by their unfamiliar surroundings.

They had both slept well. So well, that neither of them had heard the commotion during the night: the hounds baying... the clanking and crash of a drawbridge being let down... the long, slow clatter as its chains were re-wound onto the windlass. "THE STEWARD IS ABOUT TO ADDRESS US," concluded the cookney. "So I should hurry up if I was yow."

Scrambling fully clothed out of bed, the newcomers hastened to join the crowd that was gathering in the courtyard. Uncomfortable in the presence of twenty-odd strangers, they sidled up beside the cookneys – who ostentatiously chose to ignore them. There were no other women in sight – which could have been the reason behind the foot soldiers' smirks and winks. Standing slightly apart from everyone else, half a dozen darkly-clothed men stood huddled in quiet conversation.

Jacob pointed to a large, helmeted man who had emerged from the upper storey of the gatehouse and was now standing on the landing of its external wooden staircase.

"That is the Steward," the lad whispered. "He is the mon in charge here." Despite the shadow of the gatehouse walls, the man was clearly visible against their whitewashed stonework.

"I know who *that* is," snapped Gran. "I met him. Remember?"

The Steward raised a gloved hand for silence. "The Baron has brought home some good news," he bellowed, "and some not-so-good news." The congregation waited expectantly.

"As you all know, our lord and master, the Baron, has been knighted in London." After waiting for a burst of applause that didn't materialise, he continued: "Knighted by the Prince of Wales himself." Again, there was no audible response. "And now that he has returned from the celebrations in West Minster, we are to prepare a great banquet here." As a low murmur swept through the crowd, one of the cookneys muttered:

"All the more work for us. So what's the good news, then?"

As if he had overheard, the Steward raised his hand again. "The *less* good news is this: we are to raise a posse of fighting-men to help the King to bring the Scots to heel."

"What have them 'bag-carriers' ever done to *us*?" came a muted whisper from the crowd.

As its members began to disperse, the Steward's glare fell on Jacob.

"Come over here, *Boy*," he shouted. "I have something to say to thee." Jacob held back, fearful of reprisals for the incident in the Donjon.

"Yow had better go to 'im," Gran whispered, dragging him forward by the hand. "He is a *good* boy *really*," she whined as they reached the bottom of the staircase.

But instead of admonishing the lad, the Steward clomped down to ground level, took off his helmet and bent to whisper into Jacob's ear-hole.

"The Baron is going hunting today. To bring home the biggest buck in the Park."

Jacob kept his mouth shut. He was learning that he could get himself into a whole load of trouble if he didn't.

The Steward continued: "And at the Chef's insistence, I have selected *thee* to be their arrow-boy." He straightened up and re-donned his helmet. "The hunting party will assemble here in one hour, so *be ready*. Suitable attire has been taken to your quarters. *DISMISS!*" With that, the Steward pivoted around on his heel and marched purposefully off towards the Donjon.

*

The hour was almost up when the hunting-party began to assemble beside the gatehouse staircase. However, Jacob was still squatting miserably on the bake-house step. He was very proud of his fine green jerkin and pantaloons – but not so impressed with the footwear that had arrived with them. These were the first boots that he had ever been given, but their leather was so stiff that he couldn't squeeze his feet in… no matter how hard he tried.

The first to arrive at the gate had been a tall young man who strutted up and down as though he owned the place. Perhaps he did: for he wore a splendid golden cloak – emblazoned with the two blue lions of the De Somerys and trimmed around with fur. This edging, together with the broad fur collar about his shoulders and the peaked cap upon his head, were all dyed to the same azure-blue colour.

Almost immediately, a groom had led out the biggest horse that Jacob had ever seen and helped his master to mount. As Jacob watched with ever-increasing panic, a second young man slouched up. More soberly dressed than the first, something about his gait suggested that he wasn't keen. The mounted man turned to greet the newcomer – who kept his gaze averted as he vaulted unassisted into the saddle of a slightly smaller stallion.

Just as Jacob succeeded in forcing the first of his boots onto an unhappy foot, the attention of both riders became focused on three young ladies who were emerging from the gatehouse passage – all sitting sideways on fine white palfreys. Their dresses and horse-trappings gleamed in red, blue or gold, with pie-shaped hats in matching colours upon their heads.

As Jacob finally managed to pull-on the second boot, a pair of dog-handlers hurtled out of the kennels on the opposite side of the courtyard. The men halted at a respectful distance from the nobles, restraining their impatient hounds with tugs and curses. From the way they kept looking across at the riders, they were waiting for a signal of some sort.

That signal turned out to be a single blast from a horn. With the clatter of hooves on cobblestones, the party began to move off, the hounds straining against their leashes as they surged into the lead. But to Jacob's utter surprise, the party did *not* disappear into the gatehouse tunnel. Instead, they headed directly away from it, on a course that would take them right past the bakery… where Jacob was now attempting to do up his laces. In desperation, he leaned back into the doorway and called into the dark interior:

"Hey, Gran. Come and help me with these boots will yer? If yow doh, I shall be in big trouble again."

As soon as his grandmother had tied nice bows at the side of his boots, Jacob sprang to his feet and sprinted after the hunting party. Yet he had not gone more than a few paces before he was forced to slow down; his feet were killing him. How was he supposed to keep up with horse-riders when he was wearing boots that didn't fit? Uncertainty assailed him: was he *really* supposed to be going along with them? After all, nobody had taken the slightest notice of him as yet.

As he limped along dispiritedly, a larger shadow enveloped his own and a massive black horse trotted up alongside.

"Stay, lad!" The command had come from behind and above him.

"Come up and sit in front of me." An oldish-looking man was bending low over his horse's neck and proffering a leather-gloved hand. The man was clad from his hat to his boots in green leather, and he had a merry twinkle in his eyes. "You will need all of thine energy for chasing after arrows," he said, "once we get to the hunt." Chuckling to himself, the rider hauled the lad up and settled him gently onto the saddle in front of him. "The gentry will loose plenty of *them,* once they see the quarry."

As the horse lumbered into motion, Jacob quailed at the unaccustomed undulations beneath him. However, with such solid support for his back and a strong arm on either side, he quickly came to enjoy the experience. After all: he was sitting astride a real, actual, war-horse at last.

As they fell into line behind the other riders, the man revealed that he was the Baron's Chief Forester – and therefore responsible for the success of the whole expedition.

"But what am *I* supposed to do?" wailed Jacob.

"Just do as I tell thee and everything will be all right," said the Forester soothingly. "And by the way: call me *Maitre*."

"My name is *Jacques*," lied Jacob emphatically.

"Aye lad, I know it," said the Forester, nudging with his elbow. "We have *all* heard about *Jacques o' beans*." He chortled to himself for a while, before clearing his throat and continuing: "Apart from the Baron's recent knighthood, thou art the chief topic of conversation in the castle. And I hear that they are even singing a song about thee in the taverns."

By now, the other riders had disappeared into the tunnel of the North-gate – with not even a single backward glance to see if their lackey was following on behind.

"Where are we going, *Mairter*?" enquired Jacob – partly to change the subject, but more out of curiosity about their destination. Up until then, he had known only his own village of Netherton and the hilltop town of Dudley. Everywhere else was unknown territory.

"The Old Park," announced the Forester as he urged his horse into a canter. "I have already sent the limners out to locate the deer."

Jacob didn't ask what the limners were: he was too busy clinging on for dear life.

From her bake-house window, Jacob's grandmother watched her grandson's departure with mixed pride and anxiety. A shiver ran down her spine, for Jacob had a nasty habit of getting into scrapes. But he couldn't come to any harm this time... not with all that fine company... *could* he?

As she returned to her pastry-table, she noticed the cookneys – peering out through the open doorway with envy in their eyes. Only it wasn't envy at all; it was pity. Since the last arrow-boy had got an arrow in his back, no one else would touch the job with a pikestaff – let alone a quarterstaff. Of course, if they had been *ordered* to go, they would have had no choice. Thankfully, it was the newcomer who was being taken into the firing line… God help him.

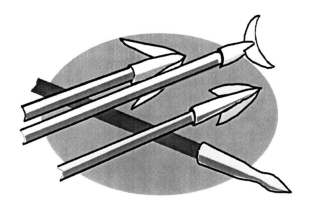

CHAPTER SEVEN

"Vwa-*lah!*" announced the Forester, nudging the lad who was perched in front of him. "Yonder lies the 'Old Park'. The hunting-ground of the gentry."

Even from his elevated position on the horse, all that Jacob could see was a hawthorn hedge and a stream which fronted it as a moat.

Startled by their approach, a heron flapped noisily into the air. Immediately, the arrogant young man rode forward with a strung bow in his hand and an arrow nocked to the string. He let the arrow fly and despite the considerable crosswind, the projectile slammed into the bird's wing. The heron fell slowly down towards the stream, spiralling around the falling arrow like a jester's bladder on a stick. Immediately, one of the hounds bounded into the water to retrieve the struggling bird – leaving the arrow to float away downstream.

"Now is thy chance," muttered the Forester as he hauled the lad bodily off the saddle and lowered him to the ground. "Hurry up! Nobles do not like to be kept waiting."

As Jacob splashed into the pebble-strewn shallows, he could appreciate (for the first time) the leather soles of his boots. Moreover, icy-cold water was leaking in through the lace-holes, simultaneously softening the uppers and soothing away the soreness from his toes.

In no time at all, Jacob had the arrow in his grasp and was hurrying back along the bank towards the riders. The arrowhead was unlike any that he had ever seen before: shaped like a crescent moon and as sharp as his grandmother's razor. Just in front of the golden-coloured flights, two tiny lions had been burnt into the shaft,

"Yes! That *is* the Baron's mark," the Forester confirmed as he hoisted the lad back into the saddle. "Be sure to recognise it from now on."

The Baron was the first to ford the stream, and the first through a gate in the hedge which had been opened by one of the men from the castle. In line astern, the other members of his party followed him through. Last of all came the Forester and his diminutive charge. After crossing a boundary ditch via a bridge of riven logs, they were in the Park.

The Forester dug his elbow into Jacob's side once more. "Thou art privileged, Jacques," he said. "Few can enter here without incurring dire penalties."

To their left, a hummocky meadow sloped up to a skyline which to Jacob seemed strangely flat.

"That is the backbone of all England," the Forester said, noticing the direction of lad's gaze. "And a feeble backbone it is as well," he added with an ironic little laugh. "No wonder the country's in such a sorry state."

Although Jacob had no idea what his mentor was talking about, he did know something about pigs.

"I know what a backbone is," he said cheerfully. "It's what my Gran puts in a stew. But it don't look straight like that."

"In this case it means a dividing line," said the Forester curtly. "All the streams on *this* side run into the Trent and thence to the North Sea... and all those on the *other* side flow into the Severn and the Western Sea." Suddenly noticing how far the nobles were in front, he spurred his horse into faster motion. "Along the... top of that... ridge," he added jerkily, "runs the... high road to Hampton. And beyond that... lie the lands controlled by... enemies of the Baron."

"The Baron has enemies, Mairter?" Jacob asked as soon as the horse slowed down again.

"Many! Nobles who are jealous of his high standing with the king. Now keep quiet will you? This next bit will require all my concentration."

With Jacob struggling to contain his curiosity, the procession of riders made their way carefully up a steepening slope of clay and loose rubble.

By reaching the top, they gained a shoulder of high ground. Rising gently up to their left, it fell off sharply to their right and in front. The nobles halted their mounts on the crest of this promontory, thus allowing the Forester to ride past. The land spread out before them was unlike anything that Jacob had seen before. The ridge they were on seemed to be acting as some kind of dam – holding back a sea of woodland which stretched away to a pair of hills on the distant horizon.

"That is where we are heading," said the Forester, pointing out over the treetops.

Although it hadn't rained for several days, the slope below them looked muddy and treacherous.

"Wouldn't it have been better to go around by that way?" Jacob asked, staring down into the tree-filled valley on their right. "That would have saved us having to climb up and down these horrible slopes."

Instead of taking offence at the lad's impudence, the Forester chuckled. "If we *had* gone round that way," he announced, "I wouldn't be able to do... this." Whilst speaking, he had been tugging on a leather strap which lay over his shoulder. Retrieving his hunting-horn, he put this to his lips and blew upon it three short blasts. And since the open end of the instrument was right next to Jacob's ear-hole, he jumped three times in quick succession.

The horse beneath them took no notice of the noise at all. She just stood there, glumly surveying the forthcoming descent as if looking for pitfalls.

Three faint notes drifted back across the treetops.

"Your ears will be better than mine," the Forester said. "Where did that call come from?"

"Over there," said Jacob, pointing. "The hill on the right, I think."

"Hurst Moor Hill?" laughed the Forester. "It would be a mighty man indeed who could blow a horn loud enough to carry *that* far." As Jacob blushed with embarrassment, he continued kindly: "My huntsmen will be much closer than that. And now that we know their direction, we shall undoubtedly learn more as we go along."

Kicking with his heels, the Forester wheeled his horse around in a tight half-circle to face the nobles. They had now arranged themselves across the crest of the ridge, their brightly coloured garments fluttering in the breeze. While the horses pawed impatiently at the ground, their riders sat watching their servant in amused silence.

Bowing from the waist (and by so doing, forcing Jacob to do the same) the Forester raised his right forearm in salutation.

"I know which one of them is the Baron," whispered Jacob, stifling a snigger, "but who am them others?"

"Be quiet, lad," hissed the Forester. "I shall tell thee later." Hoisting himself up on his stirrups, he inhaled deeply.

"Sir John… my Lord Roger… and my Ladies," he bellowed over Jacob's unruly head. "My huntsmen have been scouring the Park to ensure ye of good sport and they have now located the quarry." He waved his arm to indicate the ocean of mottled green behind him. "But first, if you will permit me, I shall guide ye to a sheltered and most pleasant glade." He paused, but receiving no response, continued unabashed: "And there, according to our most-ancient and honourable custom, music, meat and wine shall be provided for your pleasure. And come Undrentide, all shall be ready for the chase."

"Good Forester," cried the Baron, spurring his horse a few steps forward. "As always on these occasions: we must obey thy commands." He bowed low over his stallion's fluttering mane, sweeping off his cap to reveal a stubble of closely cropped hair. Without straightening up, he raised both arms out to the side in mock servility. "Lead on, Master Forester," he cried.

Thus demoted to a subordinate position, the second young man sat uneasily on his horse, scowling at the ritual that was being re-enacted in front of him. Although there was a noticeable resemblance between these two men, the second rider sat shorter in the saddle by a head – his shoulder-length hair tousled constantly by the gusting wind.

At his side, the three ladies sat respectfully on their palfreys. Jacob stared at them open-mouthed. He hadn't known that any women could look as lovely as these – with their dresses glowing red, blue and gold and their blonde hair wafting out from beneath their matching caps. And they were smiling at *him*. He looked away, disturbed by the mental image that had flashed before his eyes. For on the way to the Park, he had seen them leaping their horses over a fallen tree-trunk, while still *sitting sideways on their horses*. Clearly, he still had a lot to learn about women.

The ceremony concluded, the Forester turned his horse and began to lead the little party down towards the isolated hawthorn bushes that acted as sentinel outliers to the woods.

Jacob was no stranger to the woods. In fact, he had spent most of his spare time playing in them. But *those* woods had been twiggy willows and hazel bushes – nothing like the giant trees that confronted him now. Each was as tall as a church tower and so far round that it couldn't be girdled by a grown mon's arms. And they were so close together that as their shade enveloped him, he could scarcely make out the muddy ground beneath them. Jacob shrank back into the protective embrace of the Forester's arms. What unknown dangers might be lurking down there amongst the dark tree boles? Dragons? Goblins? Dog-headed men? There could be almost anything!

"There is no need to worry, lad," the Forester whispered. "Nothing can harm you here."

Jacob was not convinced. "We should have gone round that other way," he muttered as the horse beneath them skidded for the umpteenth time.

"Oh do shut up!" snapped the Forester as he urged his horse to cross a rivulet of running water which ran trickling down its self-cut channel. Jacob lapsed into uneasy silence, aware now that there was a limit to how much of his cheek his master would tolerate.

But after only a few minor mishaps, they vacated the brooding silence of that dark vale and emerged to level ground and bright open air. The brook that they had been following was now joined by another flowing down from their left. Nevertheless, the enlarged stream continued to run northwards – sunlit down its entire length, or as much of it as could be seen before it disappeared from sight amongst the trees that fringed its banks.

Without hesitation, the Forester rode across the stream and up through its fringe of reeds to gain the dryness of its left-hand bank. But while leading the party along a scarcely visible track, he grew increasingly fidgety.

"Take over, wiltow?" he said at last, handing Jacob the reins. "I need to reach something from my saddle-bags."

Jacob promptly forgot all his worries. So he was not in trouble after all. He was even being given the chance to steer a real actual *war-horse.*

Behind them, the little party of nobles trotted in line-astern – consenting for the time being to be led by their minion – or rather (and unbeknown to them) by a mere arrow-boy. And while the men rode in concentrated silence, the women had long-since resumed their chattering.

Since the way ahead was free of obstacles, Jacob had little to do but tug experimentally on one or other of the reins – neither of which produced any noticeable results. Nevertheless, he was in his element... until the Forester finally buckled-up his saddlebags and turned to face forward again. The intermittent pressing of the man's thighs against his own had continued all along, *and it had not stopped.*

"I thought that *I* was doing the steering," the lad complained indignantly.

"Well so you were," muttered the Forester, "in a way. But never mind that now. I promised to tell thee about the gentry. No! *Do not look around.* As you already know, the foremost rider is John de Somery – lord of the castle and all the lands here-abouts." Under his breath, he added: "Although many would dispute the extent of his grasp." After pausing to negotiate an isolated slab of grey stone, the Forester resumed his introductions: "Riding behind the Baron is Roger, his younger brother. As you may have noticed, Lord Roger is not a happy man." Jacob nodded in confirmation. "It's not surprising," the Forester continued, "since he and his mother (the Lady Agnes) have been running the Dudley estate for years. But the elder brother is back on the scene, taking over the reins and making *quite* sure that everybody knows it. And those three women are just friends of the family. Ah! Here we are."

So saying, the Forester turned his horse away from the stream and led the riders up into a seemingly untouched part of the forest. The air grew calm and still, the sighing of the wind in the topmost branches almost inaudible as thickening foliage gradually replaced dappled sunlight with shade – and ferns with leaf mould. A blackbird's alarm-call shattered the silence, echoing back from the dark tree-boles.

Eventually, they emerged into a bright and sun-lit glade, whose close-cropped turf was dotted-about with tufts of golden dandelions. Around the bushy margins, hazy drifts of bluebells added their air of mystery to the scene.

"This is the place that I have selected, my Lord," cried the Forester, reaching for his horn and blowing two short notes upon it. These were not so ear-piercingly loud as to startle his young passenger, but they were loud enough to prompt a flurry of activity in the undergrowth on the opposite side of the clearing. Out into the sunlight scrambled a young couple, both of them looking flustered and dishevelled. The youth clutched a long-necked musical instrument whose body resembled a cloven wine-keg. At his side, the wench was struggling under the weight of two heavy baskets. But in no time at all, the pair had spread out a white table-cloth on the grass, arranged jugs and plates on it, and then dashed back among the trees for further provisions.

"Your refreshments, my Lord," announced the Forester, not quite managing to conceal the relief in his voice. Noticing Jacob's keen interest in the picnic preparations, he gave his arm a squeeze. "Be patient, my lad," he said kindly. "There will be meat and ale for thee when we reach my huntsmen."

To the quietly-plucked notes of the gittern, and the girl's singing 'Soommer is a Coomen' I-h-hin', the Forester turned his horse away and re-traced his steps back down to the stream. In silence, they followed its course until it lost itself among the reed beds of a wide expanse of marsh. With the horse up to its fetlocks in dark squelchy mud, they skirted the edge of the bog, forded yet another stream, and set off up the slope towards Hurst Moor Hill. Aware that his host was periodically leaning over to his right, Jacob guessed that he must be inspecting the ground for something. But what was it? The leaf-mould passing beneath them looked just the same as any other.

"Bin yow looking for something, Mairter?" he asked.

The Forester pointed across towards a tuft of extra-long grass.

"But there is nothing there!" exclaimed the lad. "It's just grass."

"Nay! Not there! Down THERE!"

In front of the tuft, a forked twig lay flat upon the ground. It was pointing up the slope in front of them... at what seemed to be an unbroken line of hedging. "Hang on," warned the Forester as he shook the reins to urge his horse into a gallop.

With the beast pounding jarringly beneath him, Jacob watched with steadily mounting horror as the hedge grew ever-closer. He shut his eyes and clung tightly to the Forester's arms as, with a heart-stopping lurch, the horse left the ground. His stomach was still trying to find its way up his windpipe when the animal landed with a crash and a clatter. A few more strides and they were airborne again. Another teeth-clenching landing, and the Forester was reining his mount back into a trot. "How did thee like that?" he chuckled as they trotted peacefully along as if nothing untoward had happened.

Jacob opened his eyes and looked around him. "W-w-what was that?" he gasped.

"The road between the Leys of Segges and Brade," explained the Forester.

"Yow was lucky that nobody was walking along there," Jacob spluttered – immediately biting his tongue in case he had spoken out of turn again.

"That could not happen," was the unconcerned reply. "The road has been closed-off for the day of the hunt. In fact, this whole area has been cleared, even down to the wood cutters." Jacob hadn't noticed it before, but the rhythmical 'thwack' of axe striking timber had ceased the moment they entered the Park.

They were now climbing through dense woodland again. On either side, stately Elmen trees towered like the grey stone columns in a cathedral, soothing both riders into a respectful silence – a silence broken only by the quiet thud of hooves and the intermittent chink of harness rings. Eventually, they reached the crest of a high wooded hill where the Forester broke his silence:

"This is all rather strange," he muttered. "The deer have never strayed *this* far before." He yanked the horse to a sudden standstill. "We are high above Ettings Hall now, and should have caught up with my men long-since. Something is amiss here. Very much amiss, I fear."

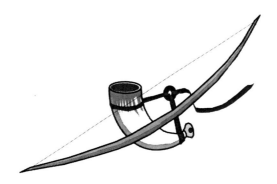

CHAPTER EIGHT

With Jacob perched in front of him, the Forester steered his horse carefully between the trees – all the while following the directions indicated by the pointing sticks. The thud of hooves had given way to a quiet rustle as they negotiated successive bumps and hollows in the spongy ground. But as they entered a particularly dark and gloomy dell, the snapping of a twig startled both riders into alertness. Out from behind a massive oak tree stepped one of the dark-clothed men from the castle – dragging a pair of reluctant hounds in his wake.

"Maitre," the man whispered as soon as he got close enough. "A strange thing has happened here."

"Well?" demanded the Forester, turning to peer questioningly into the surrounding undergrowth.

"Well, Maitre,' continued the man. "Yester-eve, we marked out a fine buck… fine enough to provide good sport and easily the best beast to grace the Baron's table." The huntsman's faltering voice betrayed his nervousness. "But when we returned this morrow-ning, we found that he had slipped away in the night... and taken all his herd with him." Moving closer, he continued in a quieter voice: "There was no mistaking which way they had gone; so clear was the spoor. So clear, Maitre, that we hardly needed to leave any pointers for you and the gentry to follow. Yow would have seen the tracks yourself."

"Aye," replied the Forester. "They are clear enough. But I had been wondering why we were being led on such a merry dance."

"It almost seemed as if we were *meant* to follow them," muttered the huntsman.

"Didestow see any sign of human activity?" snapped the Forester. "*Poachers*, for instance?"

"Nay, Maitre! Nothing like that."

"Hmm!" murmured the Forester, stroking his chin between his thumb and forefinger "So where is this splendid buck now?"

"The other limners have marked out the herd." The huntsman tugged hard on the leashes to prevent his hounds from hurtling-off in the direction of his pointing finger. "They are through there and but a furlong hence."

"And thou art sure that there is no one else near-by?"

"No one that we have seen, Maitre. And the deer seem quite undisturbed."

"Right!" said the Forester decisively. "I shall return to meet the gentry." As he helped the lad down from his horse, he added: "Give Jacques something to eat, wiltow? He will nay get any other chance until this business is finished. And see to it that he comes to no harm. Mine own lad would have been about *his* age, had he lived."

Crossing himself, the Forester rode away – leaving Jacob to tuck into the huntsman's food and ale.

Tethered to a nearby tree, a packhorse pawed disconsolately at the ground. Along each of its sides hung a row of long canvas bags – each carrying a different symbol and each showing the protruding flights of arrows.

"How will I know which arrow is which?" Jacob enquired of the huntsman, who was now sitting with his back against the tree-trunk and drinking deeply from a leather bottle.

"Just bring 'em back here and spread 'em out on the ground," mumbled the huntsman after wiping his mouth on his sleeve. "The gentry will find their own. They are good at *that*."

Jacob tugged one of the arrows from its bag and examined it closely.

"I've never seen a point like this before," he remarked to his disinterested guardian. The arrowhead was not blunt, like the ones he had seen at the butts. Nor was it crescent-shaped for winging a bird. This one had finger-length cutting blades which swept backwards into lethal-looking barbs.

"Them's for killing the deer," muttered the huntsman. "Yow take good care not to cut thyself."

Scarcely had Jacob thrust the arrow back into its bag, when the hunting party arrived with the Forester in their van. Alongside the horses, the dog-handlers ran. And these hounds looked as though they were ready to tear the whole forest apart to get at their prey.

Once each rider had selected a bag of arrows, he or she received a strung bow from the huntsman and casually nocked an arrow to its string. They paused.

Except for the snorting of the horses and the quiet clinking of their trappings, not a sound broke the silence. It seemed as if the forest around them was holding its breath.

At a blast from the Forester's horn, the hounds were released and the party exploded into motion. Horns brayed and hounds bayed as the riders weaved their horses between the trees – ducking to avoid any overhanging branches. Screaming "Soo Hooweh", they held their bows at the ready as they hurtled along. Jacob guessed that the men must be steering their mounts with their knees, like the Forester had done. But how the women were managing it was a complete mystery.

Although Jacob was running as fast as he could, he was falling ever further behind with each step. And by the time he caught up with the nobles, the hunt was pretty much over. The stag was indeed a magnificent beast, but its wide spread of antlers had become enmeshed in a curtain of netting which had been strung-up between the bushes. Staggering about on its three serviceable legs, the beast struggled valiantly to tear itself free. Around it, the hounds strained against their leashes in a semi-circle of baying malevolence.

And behind them, the riders sat silently on their horses – each with an arrow nocked to the bow in readiness. It looked magnificent... a scene from one of the stories that Jacob had been brought up on... apart from the expressions in the nobles' eyes. Jacob was accustomed to the cruelty of slaughter-men when they came to butcher his grandmother's pigs. But *these* men looked almost regretful – as if they were ashamed of having driven this magnificent beast to meet such a treacherous death. On the other hand, the women seemed to be enjoying the stricken stag's distress. Eyes bright with blood lust and teeth bared in exultant anticipation, there was no trace of pity there.

Jacob recalled the time when his grandmother had scooped up a mouse on her shovel and tossed the poor creature into the oven. He could still hear its single pitiful squeak. In spite of what he had been told about women being the gentler sex, they could be cruel. Just like everybody else.

Sickened in his stomach, Jacob left them to it. Anyway, he had been bostin' for a piddle ever since they entered the Park, and now he had his chance. Taking cover behind a massive tree trunk, he relieved himself against the bark; occasionally peeping out to make sure that none of the women could see him. But he hadn't quite finished when a single loud blast on a horn cut him off short. He peered out again – just in time to see the arrows released. Five deadly shafts sped across the clearing to hide their shiny heads in the terrified animal's hide… and one other.

Springing from a thicket to Jacob's right, it arced swiftly towards the Baron's back. Catching sight of the fast-approaching missile, the Baron's brother raised his arm – possibly in an instinctive attempt at deflecting the arrow. Instead, it skidded off his upraised bow and plunged into his own chest. After the dull thwack of the impact, the young man crumpled in his saddle and slumped sideways.

Jacob didn't see what happened next, for his eye had been caught by something moving in the thicket. A man was silently backing out from it – taking great care to prevent his bow from snagging on the twigs. But as the assassin turned to slink away, he caught sight of the horrified lad, staring at him from behind the tree-trunk. The man paused, and with only a quick glance back at the riders, put a finger up to his lips.

Jacob couldn't move, or even cry for help as the man crept stealthily towards him – drawing a murderous-looking dagger from its sheath as he came. Just in time, the power came back into the lad's legs and he was off – dashing up the slope and dodging among the trees. But in swerving round a mighty oak, he tripped over an exposed root. At first, he thought that he was done for – but somehow, his momentum kept him going forward. Recovering his balance, he staggered on – even gaining a little speed from the encounter. His pursuer wasn't so lucky. Hearing a crash and an oath behind him, Jacob glanced back over his shoulder. The assassin was down on his knees, scrabbling for the bow which had fallen from his grasp, and glaring after him with loathing in his eyes. After that, there was more running… and climbing… and even more running.

Jacob was tiring fast and the curses of his pursuer were getting nearer. By now, he had gained the crest of the ridge, where the trees were sparse enough to allow him fleeting glimpses of the castle as he ran. But even those brief sightings were enough to leave a lasting impression of gleaming white towers and walls… and safety. He scampered down the slope, confident that he was heading in the right direction, even though the assassin was presumably still close on his heels.

Reaching the temporary cover of a projecting limestone outcrop, Jacob ducked behind it and scrambled back up the slope towards a distant clump of trees. He had just decided that his ruse had worked, when an arrow whipped silently over his head. He threw himself sideways and crouching low, zigzagged towards the cover of the trees. But just as he reached the first of them, an arrow skidded off its bark and shot off into the bushes. Not long before, he had witnessed a stag being hunted to its death. Now it was *his* turn.

Another quick glance behind him and Jacob was among the trees – dashing for his life and ever fearful of an arrow in his back.

CHAPTER NINE

Suddenly, he heard a low whistle. As far as he could tell, it had come from the dark shadows in front of him. Should he keep running forwards or turn aside? But before he had time to make up his mind, urgent hands were beckoning him on.

"Here, boy," called a man's voice. "Yow get up here and drop down into the hole at the top."

He could now make out two men with their arms outstretched towards him. Although they wore dark, scruffy-looking clothes they seemed friendly enough. Behind them stood a high mound of earth, with smoke pouring out of its summit.

"But I shall be burnt alive," Jacob gasped as eager hands grabbed him and thrust him up towards the belching orifice.

"No yow woh," came the answer. "We'n owny just lit it. Just stamp out the flames and yow'll be all right."

"Here," said a second voice. "Wrap this scarf around yer gob."

In spite of his panic, one part of Jacob's chaotic mind recognised that history was repeating itself. The scarf would give him some protection from the fumes. But the thought gave him little comfort as he slid over the edge and dropped into the dark, smoking maw of the mound. As flames licked his boots, he did his best to stamp them out while battling to suppress the cough that would betray his hiding-place. He heard shouting, but it was too far away to distinguish the words. Or the muffled replies. Then there was more shouting. This time it was nearer.

"See for yower-self!" The speaker must be standing within a few feet of the mound. The silence returned.

After what seemed an age… and now fearful of being smoked like one of his grandmother's hams… the silhouette of a tousled head blotted out the disc of mottled daylight above him.

"It is safe for yow to come out now," the head whispered.

Jacob needed no second bidding. In a trice, he had scaled the funnel of smouldering twigs and was rolling down the outside of the mound.

"What was that all about?" asked one of the men as he heaped soil onto Jacob's smouldering boots.

"I have just seen somebody killed," gasped the lad.

"Oh arr! And *who* might that have been?"

"The Baron's younger brother."

"The *Baron* did yow say? The Baron of Dudley?"

"Arr."

"Hell fire!" The charcoal-burner's cautious whisper had changed into an anguished cry as he crossed himself furiously with a smoke-blackened finger. "We shall be for it if they catches yow here with us."

"Why?"

"Because the Baron is hated in these here parts. That is *why*! And if our master catches up with yow, yer life woh be worth one silver penny."

"Not even a farthing," muttered the second charcoal-burner.

"But what can I do?' wailed Jacob.

"Get out of here. And fast."

"But which way shall I go?"

"Goo back where yer come from. To the South."

Jacob peered wildly around at the dark and featureless undergrowth. "How dun I know which is the South?"

"It is not long past mid-day. Just keep the sun in front of yow and run like the wind."

"But what about that bowman?"

"Oh, *him*! We sent him off towards the Badger-ridge. It should be some time before he comes back. If he ever *does* come back...

Jacob was off – darting among the trees like a startled fawn. In front of him, the sunlight glittered down through the leaves. "That... way... safety... lay." Already, his breath was coming in short gasps. "Could... it... still... be... only... the middle... of the... day?" It seemed as if an age had gone by since he had been woken up that morning.

Suddenly, he was out in the open again – a grassy corridor which stretched into the distance on either hand. Fortunately, nothing was moving... except for a bunch of crows that were arguing noisily in the treetops on the opposite side of the ride. Below the squabbling birds, the impenetrable shadow of the wood was no longer something to be frightened of; it offered him sanctuary. Thankfully, he crashed headlong into the underbrush, kicking aside the ferns and twisting to avoid the brambles that threatened to trip him up. Yet he had barely gone a hundred paces when he heard a shout behind him. Looking round, he was horrified to see a mounted and fully armoured knight entering the wood. And close behind him: foot soldiers whose swords and spears glinted as they hacked their way into the undergrowth.

For a moment, Jacob stood transfixed as the knight thundered towards him. Armour shone like silver in the fragmented sunlight. Hooves thundered on the peaty ground. A glistening sword was held low and ready for the death-thrust.

As Jacob backed away, his heel struck against something hard. He fell backwards across a rocky outcrop. Scrambling to his feet, he vaulted the exposure and found to his horror that he had jumped over the edge of a cliff. Fortunately, he only dropped a couple of yards before his feet sank up to the ankles in a scree of loose limestone rubble. With the rattle of tumbling stones in his ears, he was carried gently down the slope – just about managing to maintain his balance. And as he descended, he glimpsed the knight above him – teetering on the edge of the cliff and shaking his sword ineffectually against the leaf-speckled sky. Of the foot soldiers, there was no sign.

Halfway down the scree-run, there was a sudden commotion below him. The four surviving members of the hunting party appeared – reining their horses into a line abreast. Each had an arrow nocked onto the bowstring and was aiming high.

Once more, Jacob noted the ladies' implacable stare, but this time he was glad of it. Shafts sped silently over his head – and from behind him came the clatter of arrowheads on iron. One… two… three… four of them. All had hit home. And suddenly, it was all over. Either the knight had been killed or he had retreated. Either way, he had gone.

"There are foot soldiers up there as well," Jacob gasped out as he stepped onto solid ground. Suddenly, the Forester was at his side and hauling him up onto his saddle again.

"Thank God we got here in time," he cried as he wheeled his horse around to follow the Baron's company into the shelter of the trees. Once beyond bow-shot, the riders formed themselves into an outwardly-facing square to resist any anticipated attack.

"I was all right, really," muttered Jacob, almost convincing himself that it was the truth. "But how did you know where to find me?"

"Lord Roger has been struck down by an arrow," groaned the Forester, "and he has since died." His arms tightened around Jacob's narrow waist. "And when you disappeared, we assumed that you had filched a bow... taken a pot-shot at the deer... and hit Lord Roger by mistake."

"But it were-nay me!" cried Jacob in horror.

"We know that *now*," admitted the Forester, "for as soon as we had withdrawn the arrow from Roger's chest, we could see that it was not one of ours. We sent the limners out to track you down. One of the handlers reported back that they had found blood on the roots of a tree and that they were tracking thee in the direction of Baggeridge." After pausing to make sure that there were no untoward sounds coming from the undergrowth, the Forester resumed his account: "And then we saw a flock of crows take fright up on that ridge and came to investigate. The rest you know. But whoever *did* loose that arrow remains a mystery to us."

"I know who it was," Jacob blurted out. "I saw him."

Immediately, Jacob was face to face with the Baron. But it was a very different Baron now. Gone was his air of haughty self-assurance. His dark-rimmed eyes followed every move of Jacob's little mouth as he did his best to describe what he had seen. And yet his efforts turned out to be disappointingly unhelpful, for the assassin had displayed no distinguishing features.

However, when Jacob went on to describe the mounted knight, he *was* able to recall something of significance: the man had been brandishing his sword in his *left* hand.

"Walter de Wynterton!" cried the Baron. "I bet my spurs that it was he. I know of no other left-handed knight. By God and all his saints, he shall pay dearly for this villainy."

Cautiously, the little party made its way back to the spot where the huntsmen were still standing guard over the dead brother's corpse. After draping Roger respectfully across his horse, they turned for home – ever mistrustful of the dark woods around them.

Vacating the park by the gate they had entered by, they made their unhappy way across to the Priory of Saint James – where they yielded-up the corpse into the tender care of its solemn, black-robed monks. As a solitary bell began to toll the death-knell, the Forester crossed himself.

"There will be non-stop praying for Lord Roger *this* night," he muttered as he turned his horse towards the castle. "And much good will *that* do him."

*

As they approached his stronghold, the Baron sent word for Jacob to be brought up to him again. As the Forester's horse drew up alongside his, Sir John leaned over towards the lad and scrutinised his grubby face:

"This is a woeful day for me," he declared between clenched teeth. "But I shall bring that coward to justice." He peered deeply into Jacob's eyes, as if hoping to see a re-play of his brother's death in their depths. Shaking his head, he announced that he would be seeking the King's justice – in spite of his monarch's preoccupation with the preparations for the Scottish campaign. "But to prove my case," he continued, "I shall need *thee* to accompany me to the West-Minster." Observing the lad's lack of understanding, he added: "That is in London. We shall leave the first thing in the morning. *BE READY.*"

A nod to the Forester, and Jacob was escorted back to the centre of the troupe. The women rode silently now – one on either side of him and one to his rear – their eyes alert, their bows strung in readiness.

*

As the hunting party re-entered the castle, it was clear to everyone there that the upstart boy who called himself "Jacques" was now under the protection of the Baron's vigilant amazons.

From her bake house window, Jacob's grandmother stared up at the Donjon tower as the great De Somery banner crept slowly down its flagstaff.

When she had heard about the death of the Baron's brother, her heart had sunk – certain that her grandson had been involved in some way. But instead... there was the Baron: patting the lad on the back in an almost friendly manner. She didn't see Jacob slide down from the Forester's horse and scamper towards her – for her eyes were overflowing with tears. If only his mother had been alive to see this day.

Life could be so cruel.

On the other hand, it could also be utterly *AMAZING*.

Part Three

Jacob
in the
Undercurrents

CHAPTER TEN

"Master! Where... did... yow... say... we was ... a-gooin'?"

Jacob had to gasp out the words in time with the motion of the horse beneath him.

"How many more times do I have to tell thee, Jacques," answered the Forester over his passenger's tousled head: "To Westminster and London!"

In spite of the ache in his backside, Jacob grinned happily at his master's use of the French version of his name. It suggested that one day he might become a soldier... just like him, and like all these other fine men who were travelling with them.

Ahead of their plunging charger, half a dozen other riders were galloping their horses along a winding and dusty road. Even from the rear, they made a splendid sight. Snow-white steeds. Polished-steel helmets sparkled in the early morning sun. Bright-blue lions adorned the golden shields on their backs.

The fore-most rider carried a lance erect – its golden pennant fluttering constantly in the back-draught. As did the blue-feathered plume on the helmet of the second rider – the Baron of Dudley, on his way to seek the king's justice for the murder of his brother.

From the thunder of hooves behind him, Jacob knew that the horse that he shared with the Forester was being followed by several others. However, his master's maile-clad arms prevented him from turning around – as did the iron-plated knees that were pressing into the back of his own. This colourful procession was overtaking a queue of heavy-looking wagons, each dragged along by a pair of weary oxen.

"Are we nearly there?" shouted Jacob above the roar of iron tyres grinding gravel into dust.

"Nay, lad. For we have not long left the town behind."

Straightening-up in his saddle, the Forester looked about him. "You know this place, surely?" he said.

Because they had left Dudley Castle so early in the morning, the market place had been deserted and they had ridden through it at speed. At the market cross, they had turned abruptly left and hurtled down the road that led directly to the nearby village of Netherton. However, Jacob had been too busy clinging on for dear life to notice.

Now he gawped with astonishment. This cluster of huts was where he had lived with his grandmother... until only a short while ago. And there, up that side lane, stood her little cottage. It looked so shabby and neglected that he fell silent – ashamed that his guardian should have seen what a poor place he had come from. And ashamed of feeling ashamed!

After a short level stretch, the road began to slope downwards again. Rougher now, the riders were forced to rein-back their horses to allow them to pick their way among the stones. This was fine as far as Jacob was concerned. No longer afraid of being catapulted off the horse, he was able to gaze out over the landscape before him.

Far ahead lay the Clent Hills, crowned as always with clumps of dark woodland. He knew their outline well, but only as a far-off backdrop to his humdrum life. He had never been there. And now, they were getting closer all the time.

"Master," Jacob shouted, pointing forward. "Are we headed for the Clent Hills? Gran says there is a dead saint up there who can forgive all our sins. Gran says that I am such a bad boy that I should go and live there all the time. Gran says…"

"Give me the chance to answer," roared the Forester. "No! We shall *not* be calling on Saint Kenelm. We leave the Salt Road before we get there, when we head off east for Coventry."

"Is *that* the place where the lovely lady rode through the streets?" asked Jacob, remembering a tale his grandmother once told him, "with no clothes on?"

"So they say," replied the Forester. "And where Peeping Tom had his eyes put out for looking at her."

"Why… would he… want to… look at her… Master?"

"To see what she was like."

"But *why*?"

"You will know *that* when you are older," snapped the Forester.

For the moment, Jacob remained silent. His grandmother always fobbed him off like that. Well he was getting older all the time and he was still none the wiser.

"How long will it take us to get there?" cried Jacob.

"Coventry is about five hours' hard ride from the castle," answered the Forester curtly. "And so five hours it should take. Well it would take, if the Baron did-nay intend to call off at Weoley Castle to comfort his mother in her despair."

"Her dis... *what*, Master?"

"Her sadness! Now DO shut up!" It was one thing to be expected to take the lad all the way to London. It was quite another to have to keep answering these infernal questions. After all, he had other things to think about: like how to prevent Jacques from coming to harm. It was likely that he was still in great danger: as the only witness to the slaying of the Baron's younger brother... a murder that he (as the Baron's Head Forester) should have prevented.

All this time, a two-wheeled cart had been trundling up the hill towards them. Piled high with an enormous heap of hay, the donkey between its shafts was scarcely able to make any headway against the slope. And as if the load and the inclination weren't enough of a burden, the overweight driver sat a-top the heap, lashing at the struggling beast's flanks with his whip.

When the cart reached the rider with the lance, its pennant described a gilded arc through the air as it struck the driver full on the back – knocking him sideways off the cart. Relieved of his considerable weight, the cart immediately toppled backwards, its shafts hoisting the donkey off its feet. By the time Jacob drew level, the beast was hanging suspended in the air – braying with terror and flailing ineffectually with its hooves.

"What did he do *that* for?" cried Jacob, pointing at the knight who was now brandishing his lance and whooping with laughter.

"Thomas never *could* stand cruelty to animals," came the amused reply.

*

Occasionally, the road levelled out – usually where a huddled group of huts stood guard over strips of cultivated ground, already showing the emerging shoots of this year's crop.

"It is a great pity that they will not be harvested in time to feed the army," observed the Forester dryly.

"They might have been, if they had planted Merlin's beans," retorted the lad.

Eventually the road levelled out, reduced to half its width by a wooded slope on their left-hand side. On their immediate right, a large expanse of water reflected an even-higher hill.

"Up there lies the ville of Hales." The Forester was pointing up at the top of that hill – hazy with smoke from the cottages whose thatched roofs were dimly discernible among the treetops.

However, Jacob was too busy watching the pedestrians who were crowding in on them from both sides. At the approach of the Baron's horsemen, scruffy-looking peasants glanced up – grimaced with indignation – but then hurriedly scrambled out of the way.

"We are now in Shropshire," announced the Forester unconcernedly. "We started off in Staffordshire. Then we crossed a part of Worcestershire… and now we have entered a little bit of Shropshire. All in the space of… five miles or so."

"I did-nay notice any difference," said Jacob. "Does it matter?"

"It might do," answered the Forester thoughtfully, "*if,* as they say, Longshanks the King has not much longer to live."

Suppressing a chuckle at his unintended pun, he continued hurriedly: "And *if* his son, turns out to be as ineffective a ruler as they predict, the barons might well take up arms against him like they did his grandfather. And if that happens, who can tell where the battle-lines will be drawn?" He heaved a sigh of resignation. "We can only hope that Edward of Caernarfon will be half the man his father was… and still is, even now in the winter of his years."

Understanding little of this and caring less, Jacob allowed his eyes to scan the crowd. They registered nothing of particular interest until they met another pair – staring at him from the shadowy interior of a russet-coloured hood.

A sudden spark of recognition set his heart a-thumping. He had seen that face before. He skewed round in the saddle – leaning out and around his master to get a better look. But he was not quick enough. The man had tilted his head forward so that his face was completely hidden in shadow. Yet Jacob could still recall that wild-eyed stare. It was the stare of the man who had killed Lord Roger. And the assassin had almost certainly recognised *him* – the only witness to his dastardly deed.

CHAPTER ELEVEN

"Admiring the wenches, are we?" chuckled the Forester, nudging the lad who was fidgeting in the front of his saddle.

"No, Master," Jacob protested. "I think the man who shot Lord Roger is over there." He had spoken as loudly as he dared, and tilted his head ever-so-slightly towards the spot where the assassin still stood.

"What was that?" muttered the Forester bending forward. "I can-nay hear you above this rabble."

"That hooded man," said Jacob cautiously. "The one leaning against the gibbet. I think he is the man who shot Lord Roger."

"Shout up louder, lad," cried the Forester, deeply concerned about a deterioration in his hearing (caused by all that blowing on his hunting-horn, no doubt). Laying the reins upon his horse's neck, he carefully removed his helmet and handed it to his passenger. "Hold this, wiltow? Now, what was *that* you were saying?"

With his hands wrapped protectively around the precious helmet, Jacob tilted his head back and swivelled his eyes in the direction of the hooded man.

"That man over there," he said. "The one in the hood. I think that *he* is the one who shot the Baron's brother."

"What man?" cried the Forester, turning himself bodily round in the saddle. "I can see no man."

And it was true; the suspected killer had melted away into the crowd.

"Hang on, lad." The Forester spurred his horse through the resentful throng – pushing them aside as easily as a plough parting sandy soil. Drawing abreast of the Baron, he raised two gauntleted fingers to his temple in a respectful salute.

"My Lord," he cried above the protests. "This lad says that he has just seen Roger's killer."

"What?" cried John de Somery, reaching instinctively for his sword. "Where?"

"Back there," shouted the Forester, "but vanished among the rabble. I did-nay see him myself... but the lad says that he is sure that it was he."

"Nearly sure," interjected Jacob. "It all happened so quick."

"Right!" The Baron turned round in his saddle to address his men: "Group up around the Forester and make all speed for the Abbey."

"Oi! Watch where yow'm a-gooin!" The indignant cry had issued from the front of the Baron's horse as it lurched forward.

"Get out of my way," screamed the knight, drawing his sword from its scabbard. It gleamed like silver over his head. "Or shalltow feel my steel upon thy neck."

"I urge thee to caution, my Lord," warned the Forester, hastily riding forward. "For thou hast no jurisdiction here. These are the Abbot's lands."

"Get this rabble out of my way, then," snarled the Baron, reining-in so hard that the bit jerked his horse's head back sharply.

"Leave it to me, my Lord," cried the Forester, riding forward and bellowing out above the crowd: "Clear the way, for the Baron."

"Baron who?" shouted some anonymous citizen in the crowd.

After a short but uncomfortable gallop, an enormous gatehouse stood across their path. In contrast with the whitewashed stonework of Dudley Castle, these reddish blocks had the feel of calm serenity. Or they would have done: if it hadn't been for the noisy beggars who were encamped against the walls.

Hooves ringing on cobblestones, the Forester galloped his horse up to the great ironbound door and pummelled on it with the pommel of his sword.

"Sir John de Somery," he bellowed, "requires shelter for himself and his retinue."

At a nod, the member of that retinue who was named Thomas raised his lance to display its golden pennant. Its blue lions must have confirmed the identity of the visitors, for after only the briefest of intervals, a side door groaned open and a white-robed monk stepped out. Holding up his hand against the glare of the sun, he ignored the clamour for food that enveloped him, and turned to address the newcomers:

"On what business dostow come?"

"We claim hospitality in the name of John de Somery," cried Thomas. "The Baron of Dudley."

The Baron rode forward to take charge of the situation.

"I am en-route to see the King in Westminster," he bellowed, "and I demand an audience with Abbot Walter."

"Come in and welcome," replied the priest, smiling. With arm outstretched, he pointed towards a larger gate which a second monk was already dragging open. "Though I hear that the King may no longer be in residence there. Incidentally..." he added, "The Lady Agnes is here amongst us."

From his perch on the Forester's horse, Jacob looked down on the scene before him with wonder.

"Master," he whispered. "Why are these monks dressed in *white*, while them in Dudley all wear *black*? Are *these* the good monks and the other monks the *bad* ones?"

"Nay, lad," whispered the Forester, suppressing a chuckle. "Monks are all pretty-much all as bad as one another. These are just a different type of monk. They wear different-coloured habits to tell themselves apart."

"Like birds then?"

"Aye. Like birds if you like. And like birds: when they are not singing, they are cramming as much food down their gullets as they can swallow."

*

Once beyond the gatehouse, the riders entered a broad but shallow valley. Rounding its left-hand sweep, the Abbey itself came into view, its high-gabled walls glowing red against the wooded ridge beyond.

The Abbey was much bigger than the Priory at Dudley, but it had a similar square tower rising from its middle. In front of the buildings, a series of lakes led up the valley to a water mill whose wheel was threshing water into foam.

"That is the second mill I have seen around here," said Jacob wonderingly. "They must have a lot of corn to grind."

"Nay, lad," muttered the Forester bitterly. "This mill will be the only one around here that can grind corn. If the Abbot is as greedy as the Baron is, nobody will be allowed to take their grain anywhere else."

"What about that one under Hales Hill, then?"

"Oh! That could be used for anything. Anything other than for grinding corn."

Now that they were nearing the Abbey, its lancet-pierced walls stretched high against the sunlit sky. Reflected in the still waters of a lake, they also appeared to plunge down as far beneath the surface. "A fitting bridge between this world and the next," as the Forester described it.

"What *is* this place?" asked Jacob as they clattered over a wooden bridge towards the main building. Beside the ornate entrance, another monk stood with his arm out-stretched, apparently waiting to take charge of the horses.

"This is the Abbey of The Virgin and Saint John," muttered the Forester as he hauled Jacob bodily off the saddle and lowered him gently down to the ground. "Where the Lady Agnes will be praying for the soul of her favourite son."

"Why do that here?" asked Jacob, "when his body lies back there in Dudley Priory?"

"Because she lives nearby – in Weoley Castle – which is just over that ridge."

*

Soon, Jacob and the Forester were being shown into a sumptuously furnished apartment. Paintings of biblical scenes covered the walls. Gold-leaf embellishments glowed and writhed in the flickering light of the central fire. A strange, sweet scent filled the air.

The Lady Agnes sat slumped forward across a large wooden table, an ivory-handled knife at her elbow. Alerted by the creaking door, she looked up and immediately beckoned the pair to enter. In spite of the shadows around her eyes, she was a strikingly beautiful woman. Her dark-grey hair was almost completely covered by a square of white cloth, while her black velvet dress glistened in the firelight as she half-arose from her seat.

"Come here boy, and sit by me," she commanded, pointing a bejewelled finger at a leather-topped stool beside the table. "And tell me everything you know of my dear son's death." Her lips were contorted in an attempt at a smile, but her grey eyes shone with the cold hard glint of burnished steel.

Perching himself uncomfortably on a corner of the stool, Jacob related his account of Roger's untimely death.

The lady listened attentively, caught-up in his narrative. Unaccustomed to such exalted attention, Jacob laid it on thick. In great detail, he described how he had witnessed the arrow-shot that killed Lord Roger. As the lady rubbed her fingers together with anguish, the lad couldn't take his eyes off her rings. Their faceted gems reflected the firelight in tiny little bits, just like the Abbey's windows had done in the sunlight.

"Go on!" demanded the lady irritably.

Jacob 'went on' to describe his flight from the assassin and his subsequent rescue by the amazons: "And then they—"

"The Baron says that you have seen the assassin since," interrupted the lady. "Is this the sooth?"

"I th-think so, my lady," stammered the lad. "Although I can-nay be wholly sh-sure that it was him."

"Canstow describe him?"

"He was j-just a man," muttered Jacob, searching his memory (yet again) for some hitherto-forgotten feature which might identify the killer.

"Sported he a beard?"

"N-nay! He was c-c-clean shaven."

"Colour of hair?"

"What?" spluttered the lad.

"Do not 'what' me," snarled the lady, her expression contemptuous. "Didstow see the colour of his hair?"

"N-no, m-my lady. He wore a hood."

"Be gone then, Boy," she commanded, waving him away with a sparkling hand.

For a moment, Jacob just sat there. The great lady hadn't been interested in *him* at all. Just in what he could tell her.

"Go on then!" she urged, rising from her seat.

Disillusioned and disappointed, Jacob shuffled back to the Forester, who was waiting patiently beside the doorway.

"Come along, my lad." The man ruffled the boy's hair affectionately and then grabbed his hand to lead him from the room.

"Pick up your feet," shrieked the Lady behind them. "And for heaven's sake have a wash."

"That is good advice," chuckled the Forester to the blushing boy. "For it will soon be time to eat. And do cheer up! They say that the food here is superb – if you like bream."

CHAPTER TWELVE

Jacob was hardly able to believe his eyes. Or his ears. Or for that matter: his nose.

Having been taken up to the first-floor refectory of the Abbey, he was sitting with the Forester and the other soldiers – all waiting to be served the noon-tide meal.

Their table occupied the whole of one narrow end of the long room, while the Baron and his mother sat at a similar table at the other end. The Baron had changed his protective armour for a robe which, being bright crimson in colour, stood out like a beacon-fire in a mist. The lady Agnes was still wearing her black dress, but her throat was now veiled with a white scarf. Between them, a rotund monk sat imperiously in a high-backed chair. He was clad all in white, even up to the tall, pie-shaped hat upon his head.

Along both sides of the room, white-robed monks sat at similar tables. None of them were speaking. Instead, they were whistling at one another – all at the same time and none of them in unison or in tune. One monk even had his forefingers shoved in his mouth. His high-pitched note echoed down from a high raftered roof which arched over their heads like the upturned hull of a great ship.

Jacob sat there appalled. Grown men should-nay behave like this! His grandmother would not have stood for it for an instant, so why was-nay the monk in the pie-shaped hat putting a stop to it? Instead of putting a stop to it, he sat sprawled in his throne, drinking from a silver goblet and smacking his lips like a chicken sipping water.

The Forester leaned over to whisper into Jacob's ear:

"Your likening of monks to the birds was more fitting than I thought."

As the boy opened his mouth to reply, a chorus of ear-piercing whistles was directed in their direction. Since the blasts were accompanied by fierce glares and the pressing of fingers against lips, it was pretty obvious that they were being told to shut up. This was rich, coming from *them*! Nevertheless, the Forester raised his hands to signal his apology. There was to be no talking here, even in the midst of all that cacophony.

So Jacob sat gazing quietly up at the tall lancet wind-eyes. These were filled with squares of some kind of see-through stuff, all joined together to form glistening patchworks of light. There was something of the sort in the chapel at Dudley Castle, but that had been too high up for him to see what it was made of. Somebody had told him that the squares were called 'quarries' and that they were made of glass, but he had taken that with a pinch of sand. They looked nothing like the little fragment that he had stepped on outside his grandmother's cottage.

But with the sunlight streaming in through them, these squares did look a bit like the little shard that had given him such a nasty gash. Never one to look a gift-horse in the mouth, he had picked it up and kept it safe – using it for shaping wooden swords and arrows.

But it was the *pictures* on the wind-eyes that really amazed him. They were pictures of knights in armour – mostly with a cross in one hand and a sword in the other. As his grandmother's words came back to him, he crossed his fingers. Hopefully, the saints would preserve *him* from the killer who was lurking about outside.

At the far end of the room, the Baron was ignoring the roasted goose which had been set down before him, and was gazing up at the pictures with a thoughtful expression on his face. The monk in the pie-shaped hat was now tucking into his goose, while the lady Agnes had her knife poised and ready for the one that was being carried in her direction.

Jacob's mouth was watering. Only rarely had he been given chicken-meat to eat and never, ever, a goose.

Then he saw the cookneys; two harassed-looking young monks whose heads had not been shaved in the middle like the others. Indifferent to the raucous ribaldry around them, they began to ladle stew from a cauldron which hung from a pole on their shoulders. The smell of it was the *third* surprising thing. It was the smell of boiled fish. So he and the Forester would *not* be getting goose flesh like the nobles. Just *fish*.

Jacob was no stranger to eating fish, for his grandmother had often cooked him a roach or two for his dinner. But they had never stunk as bad as this. This stuff smelt more like the concoction she used to entice vermin into her traps.

Jacob reached up to hold his nose, but one glance from the Forester dissuaded him. He regarded the wind-eyes with much less admiration now. Blocking them up was not such a good idea after all.

*

The cookneys were still only halfway down the refectory when the monk in the pie-shaped hat leaned back in his throne and closed his eyes with obvious contentment.

Observing Jacob's interest in the heraldic shield above the monk's high seat, the Forester used his fore-finger to trace out letters in spilt beer:

'T H E   A B B O T'

Unable to make any sense of this, Jacob lapsed into an embarrassed silence.

Meanwhile, the Baron had unfolded a piece of parchment and was studying it intently.

He could read all right, Jacob thought. Prob'ly, *everybody* in this hall could read. How was *he* ever going to become a soldier if he could-nay read or write?

As the three aristocrats passed the document between themselves, one or other of them would occasionally look up and stare hard in Jacob's direction.

What was he doing wrong now? Was it wrong to be nibbling on his slice of bread? But he was *starving* and there were an awful lot of monks to be served before the cookneys would get to him. But now he came to look, the monks were all placing their pieces flat on the table to receive their dollops of stew.

Just as Jacob's dollop plopped onto a fresh slice of bread, the rasping of chairs on floorboards announced that the nobles were getting to their feet. As they turned to leave by a door behind them (which Jacob hadn't noticed before) he saw to his dismay that the Baron was beckoning for the Forester to follow. And for him to be brought along as well.

Jacob flushed with anger and disappointment. *They* had all stuffed themselves solid, and *he* hadn't even started yet. "BUT I HAVE-NAY HAD ANYTHING TO EAT!" he cried, the protest having escaped his lips before he could stop it.

Immediately, the whole refectory reverberated to the sound of whistling monks – all in unison for once. And as the cookneys dropped their cauldron, Jacob was hustled out through the doorway and into a torch-lit corridor.

*

Arriving back at the lady's chamber, the Baron swaggered across to the fire and stood with his backside to its flames. Jacob and the Forester held back, hesitating just inside the doorway.

The Baron held the document aloft.

"I am summoned to attend the King in Carlisle," he announced to the room in general. "He intends to march into Scotland and crush those rebels, once and for all."

Marching across to the heavy wooden table, he tossed the parchment onto its polished surface.

"That traitor The Bruce," he roared, "has sent the Fiery Cross around the glens. And FORCED OUR MEN TO TAKE REFUGE IN OUR CASTLES." The table boomed under the impact of his fist. "However," he continued in a more restrained voice. "These are all well-victualled, and two of Edward's most trusted earls have been sent up there to Raise the Dragon."

"What's that, Master?" asked Jacob quietly.

"Hush, lad," whispered the Forester. "I shall tell thee later. I am more concerned about how all this is going to affect us."

He didn't have long to wait, for the Baron stomped over to where he and the lad were standing. Putting his arm around the Forester's shoulders, he looked surprised at the man's flinch.

"Do not worry, Will," he murmured. "I know that you feel personally responsible for the death of my dear brother, but we *all* know who did the deed... or at least: who *ordered* it to be done."

Stepping back, he patted his servant on the shoulder. "As you well know," he said quietly. "We were on our way to Westminster to demand the King's Justice for my brother's death." He pointed to the document which still lay open on the table. "But it appears that the King is already on his way north. I am to meet him in Carlisle with all the men that I can muster."

"As always, my Lord," said the Forester, dropping to one knee, "I am at your service."

"Nay, Will," said the Baron, raising his minion to his feet. "Thou hast served the King well in the past but this battle is not for thee." He glanced down at Jacob, who was straining his ears to catch every word. "I need thee to escort this lad safely back to Dudley. Meantime, I shall accompany the Lady Agnes to Weoley to enlist her horsemen and archers for the King's service." On hearing this, his mother glowered at him from the far side of the fire.

The Forester risked a glance into his master's eyes, hoping to reassure himself of his goodwill. However, their cold and humourless expression belied the friendliness of his words.

Turning abruptly away, the Baron returned to the table and picked up the parchment. After staring at it for a while, he tossed it into the fire.

"I must have a letter en-scribed by the monks here," he said, "and sent quickly to the King (wherever he may be along the Great North Road) to demand the heads of Wynterton and his hired killers." Pausing, he sniffed the air. "By the way, what is that infernal stink?"

Blushing with embarrassment, Jacob produced his slice of bread, still wet with traces of the stew.

"For God's sake, get rid of that," the Baron commanded.

Jacob scampered across to the fire and threw his piece into the flames. As an abominable stench filled the room, its occupants were forced to make a hasty exit.

"History is repeating itself again, eh?" laughed the Forester as he escorted his mortified charge away.

*

A scattering of raindrops pattered across the roof-tiles of the gatehouse dormitory. Jacob lay back in his bed, mulling over the incredible sequence of events that had brought him to this place: from his meeting with the man who called himself Merlin in Dudley market place... to the slaying of the Baron's brother in The Old Park.

Shivering with remembered terror, he recalled his headlong flight from the assassin... who even now was less than half a mile from where he lay. But he *should* be safe enough here in the Abbey, with the Baron's soldiers to protect him. He could hear them downstairs now, laughing with the monks who were supposed to be guarding the gates. Mind you, those monks were not afraid to use weapons, if those on the walls were anything to go by. And this gatehouse looked almost as impregnable as the one at Dudley Castle. He had seen good strong walls running off in both directions, and the Forester had said that they went all the way round the Abbey grounds. Yet he had not noticed any patrols on them. And what about that millstream? It had to be let out somewhere. And where water could get out, an assassin might steal in.

Just as that thought occurred to him, he heard shuffling on the stairway that led up to his resting place. Stealthy feet were creeping up... with no accompanying candle-glow to reassure him. The assassin must have got in after all. And was *coming up to silence him.*

CHAPTER THIRTEEN

Suddenly, the footsteps stopped, the ensuing silence broken only by the quiet sound of the intruder's breathing. He must be about halfway up the staircase, with his eyes on a level with the floorboards. But nothing could be seen of him out there beyond Jacob's little sphere of candlelight.

Overcoming the paralysis of fear, he had just managed to get one leg out of bed when: "So you *are* awake."

It was the Forester's voice. And as he continued up the stairs, the candlelight revealed that he was carrying a wooden platter... piled high with slices of bread and cheese.

"I could-nay let you go to sleep on an empty stomach," explained the man, as he sat heavily on the edge of the bed.

Although brimming over with questions, Jacob was absolutely *starving*. So he crammed down the food as fast as he could. But as he swallowed the very last morsel, he could restrain his impatience no longer.

"Master," he blurted out, breadcrumbs gleaming in the candlelight as they arced down to the counterpane, "Yow promised to tell me about the Fiery Dragon. Is it a great big lizard? Is it conjured up from Hell to gobble up our enemies?"

"Nay lad," laughed the Forester, sweeping away the crumbs with the back of his hand. "You have been paying too much attention to the tellers of tall tales. The 'Fiery Cross' is what the *Scots* use to mobilise their forces for war. On the other hand, *we* fly the 'Dragon Banner' to signify that we shall give no quarter in battle. And by that I mean that we shall execute every noble who has dared to raise his hand in treason against our King... and burn his crops and raze his dwelling-place to the ground."

Jacob fell silent, unnerved by the hard edge on his master's voice.

The raindrops had now become a steady thrumming above their heads. But there, in the warm darkness of the dormitory, and guarded by the troops below, he felt secure enough to risk another question.

"Master, what did the Baron mean about you serving the King?"

It was the Forester's turn to fall silent. Eventually, he cleared his throat and began to speak – his unshed tears glistening in the candlelight.

"It must be about... eight years ago now," he began throatily. "On Saint Magdalena's day. A fitting day that was, since she is the Saint of repentant sinners. It was at a place in Scotland called Falkirk. As we approached the battle-ground, their leader (William Wallace by name) had his foot soldiers roped-off in four enormous rings."

The Forester barked his ironic little laugh. "To prevent them from running away, no doubt. Anyway, each ring was bristling with pikes like a ruddy great hedgehog, so our mounted knights could-nay get near 'em."

Jacob leaned forward, straining his ears to catch every word above the drumming rain.

"They had archers and cavalry to back them up,' the Forester continued, "but we soon put *them* to flight. And then Old Longshanks (the King) called forth his bowmen."

The Forester swallowed hard – obviously deeply affected by some inner vision. When he resumed, his voice had an even-harsher edge to it. "I was one of their marksmen. The bag-carriers didn't stand a chance. We aimed high, so that our arrows fell on them like rain. The poor baggers had no choice but to stand there and take it – struck down like ripe corn in a cloudburst."

Coincidentally, the rain outside increased in severity to become a downpour, whose torrential roar almost drowned out the Forester's next words.

"The King claimed it as a great victory, but it was more like murder." He sighed. "They were just poor farmers – left to be slaughtered while their overlords escaped into the hills."

"Could they do nothing to protect themselves?" Jacob interjected. "Had they no shields?"

"Some of them *did* have shields," admitted the Forester, "but they were-nay much use to them. At the command of King Edward himself, we marksmen would each send a fire-arrow into our chosen spot at the front of a ring. And then the other bowmen would concentrate their fire on that spot until the poor baggers collapsed under the onslaught. And then our knights would swoop in and cut the survivors to pieces. I can still hear them screaming... especially when I am just on the point of waking-up.

"Mind you," he cried, suddenly cheerful again. "They would have done the same to us, had they got the chance."

"Well, now *that* is sorted," came an indignant voice from the far end of the dormitory. "Can we all get some sleep? Some of us have got to get up in the morning."

"Actually, so have we," whispered the Forester, bending close Jacob's ear. "We start back for Dudley at the crack of dawn."

"So I am not to be taken to the King after all?"

"Nay, lad," said the Forester regretfully. "Word has it that he is travelling up the Great North Road. Even at its closest, that is many miles away from here, and we have no way of knowing how far he has travelled along it. Dudley Castle is the safest place for thee."

*

Well before the dawn of the next day, three horses were led quietly out through the Abbey gate. Fortunately, the beggars outside had not yet emerged from their makeshift tents, so the riders were hopeful of getting away unobserved.

The Forester mounted easily – hauling Jacob up to sit in front of him with an ease that denoted great strength of arm.

And with an armoured knight stationed fore and aft, they set forth on the road back to Dudley, thankful that the night's storm had at last abated. Their shields had been covered with cloth to conceal their identity, and the hooves of their horses bound up in bags of straw to muffle their impact on the wet cobbles.

It wasn't long before the riders reached the vale beneath Hales Hill. The roadway had become a sea of mud and the hillsides were awash with running water.

Jacob looked anxiously about him, fearful that the assassin might still be lurking nearby. But the road was deserted. And although the mud still held the impressions of many feet, the people who had made them had long since departed for home. The hillside on their right offered no hiding-place for a would-be killer. Rivulets and tree-trunks glistened brightly in the daylight that had begun to suffuse a cloud-flecked sky. Jacob began to relax, reassured by the cool hardness of the Forester's chainmaile against his back. Perhaps he had been mistaken. Perhaps the killer was not here after all. Why *should* he be, so far away from the scene of his crime?

He was just settling down to enjoy the steady motion of the horse, when it suddenly bucked beneath him. Braying with terror and pain, it reared up, catapulting both of its passengers off its back. As Jacob landed on his side in the mud, he glimpsed their erstwhile mount, racing away with an arrow sticking up out of its flank – the brown flights waving like a bullrush in the wind. In its panic, the injured animal leaped over the recumbent body of the leading horse, which was struggling unsuccessfully to get to its feet. Its rider lay still, in spite of repeated kicks from flailing hooves.

"Artow all right, lad?" cried the Forester, struggling to his feet. While trying to scrape the worst of the mud from his maile hauberk, he peered around for the third horseman (of whom there was no sign).

"I think so, Master," groaned the lad from the mud that had cushioned his fall. "What happened?"

By way of an answer, another arrow plunged down from the sky. Having given no warning of its descent, it was suddenly there – quivering upright in the mud between them. The Forester slithered across to the lad and pushed him forcibly down. As the man bent protectively over his charge, another arrow arrived to keep company with its mate.

"So you were right after all," the Forester muttered grimly. "The assassin really *is* here. But where is he shooting from? Both arrows are inclined away from Hales Hill, so they must have been shot from somewhere on this side." Lowering his visor to shield his eyes against the glare of the morning sun, he squinted up the nearby hill. Between the glistening tree trunks, the silhouettes of fully armoured men were slipping and slithering down the slope towards them. Fortunately, they were a long way off as yet.

"They are coming to finish us off," the Forester cried, hauling the lad to his feet and pushing him away. "Escape while you can, whilst I stay here to hold them o… AGGGHHH!" He screamed as an arrow pierced the back of his leg – parting the unriveted links of maile as easily as a finger in a bowl of peas.

The arrow came out easily to his tugging, for although the head was needle-sharp, it carried no barb. With blood spurting from his wound, the Forester rose unsteadily to his feet and drew his sword from its sheath. Or what was left of it. The weapon had snapped beneath him as he fell and only two hand-breadth's length remained of the blade. "Ruddy swordsmiths!"

Casting the useless item away in disgust, he turned to face the next shower of arrows. Yet Jacob had not been idle. Since their own shield had been smashed in the fall, he had slithered across to the fallen horse and returned with its rider's. It was scarcely big enough to cover the two of them but nevertheless, it received two more arrows as they retreated backwards towards the hill of Hales – and the stream which fronted it.

Below them, the waters of the swollen river swirled and roared between rock-strewn banks. The only way forward was down a sopping-wet, slippery mudslide.

"Hey there! Will Hawkes." The caller was some distance behind them.

Astonished, the Forester turned away from the ravine. "Who calls?" he bellowed.

"Adam Wynterton," came the reply. "Thow knowest me, surely. I fought alongside thee at Falkirk. Dostow not remember? You should, for I am the one you left behind to die."

The Forester blanched – staring hard at the silhouette of the man who was standing at the bottom of the hill. His companions were waiting higher up the slope, each clinging to a tree-trunk for support.

"I do not remember that," the Forester yelled back. "But if it is *me* thatow hast come for, let the lad go free."

"Nay, Will," came the reply. "I cannot do that, for I have come for both of thee. Two birds with one stone, ye might say."

"Make for the Abbey," muttered the Forester, giving Jacob a shove that sent him careering over the edge of the ravine.

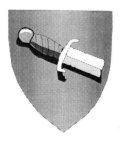

CHAPTER FOURTEEN

As Jacob slid over the edge of the ravine, he grabbed the Forester's leg.

"I'm not going without yow," he screamed, hooking his fingers into the lacings of the maile and holding on tight. As luck would have it, the leg that he was clinging on to was the Forester's uninjured one. And as the man sought to maintain his balance, his wounded leg gave way beneath his weight.

Together, the two fugitives avalanched down the slope into the swollen river. Weighed down by the Forester's maile, the muddy water immediately surged over their heads.

They surfaced, coughing and spluttering, a little further downstream. Thereafter, they were carried along like twirling logs – around successive bends of the river, and gasping for breath whenever they got the opportunity. At last, the current slowed – depositing them gently in the calm waters of a shallow pool. Overhead, the trees on opposite banks interlaced their branches to form a screening canopy of leaves. At the exit to this secret bower, the pool was discharging itself over a cascade of rapids into a larger body of water. And at the far end of this pool, a water wheel was rotating slowly – to the accompaniment of a distant: thump… thump… thumping sound.

"Quiet, lad," whispered the Forester unnecessarily. "They might think that we have drowned."

Unfortunately, they thought no such thing.

"A thousand silver pennies for the lad, and two-thousand for the man." The cry had come from immediately above the spot where the fugitives were crouching among the exposed roots of a willow tree. All too soon, the riverbank above them was swarming with enthusiastic bounty hunters.

"I am done for, lad," groaned the Forester, trying in vain to put some weight on his wounded leg. "Wait until they have passed by, and then make your way back upstream. You might even get the chance to climb up into the town. And if by some miracle you do make it, claim sanctuary in the church. Even these cut-throats will not dare to transgress that holy place." Crossing himself, he added: "Ring the tower-bell to summon help from the Abbey."

With that, he hobbled off down the rapids and plunged headfirst into the swirling waters of the millpond. The last sign of him that Jacob saw was a retreating line of bubbles breaking the surface.

"They are down here."

Following that cry, Jacob heard the swish of running feet as the would-be claimants hurried down to the millpond.

As soon as it had all gone quiet, Jacob made his move. By hanging onto tree-roots and boulders, he crawled his way back upstream against the flow. Twice, he thought that he had been spotted. And twice, he lay still and allowed the muddy water to flow over him. Although he couldn't know it, the mud on his clothes blended perfectly with the clay of the riverbank – providing the best camouflage that anybody could wish for.

At last, he reached a stretch of the river where the right-hand bank looked climbable. And even with his eyes at water level, he could clearly see the church-tower beyond the crest of the slope.

He was just about to make a dash for it, when he heard a SPLASH. It had come from just around the next bend. He froze. Then came a series of rhythmic splashes, accompanied by a badly-whistled tune. It sounded like a washerwoman – come down to the river to do her laundry. In spite of his desperate predicament, Jacob smiled wryly to himself: any washerwoman who would put up with that muddy water could not be very particular.

He risked a peep around the corner and saw, not a washerwoman – but a youth kicking boulders into the stream. Jacob ducked back into cover, but the movement caught the youth's eye.

"He is here," the youth whooped. "I claim the reward."

Jacob was off, scrambling up the bank towards the church. But no matter how much he clawed at the mud, he kept slipping back.

"Come and get him," cried the youth from immediately behind him. "He is still here."

With the church so tantalisingly close and yet so far beyond his attainment, Jacob turned angrily on the youth and pulled the broken-off sword from his belt. He had never been one to pass *any*thing by, which might come in handy later.

Eyes wide with alarm, the youth backed-away up the stream.

"Get away from me," he whimpered.

"Keep your mouth shut then," growled Jacob, turning on his heel. Aware that the youth's accomplices would be hurrying to the spot, he dashed back down the river – splashing through its shallows and letting himself be swept along in its deeper, stronger stretches. Soon, he had sprinted down the rapids and was diving headfirst into the mill-pool. Once more, he felt the shock of the ice-cold water, but this time he was alone.

Weighed down by the broken sword, he was carried along the bottom by the undertow. He had no fear of drowning, for swimming was his joy (encouraged by his grandmother as the only way to get him to bathe). As usual, when he opened his eyes underwater there was nothing to see but brown murky water. But never before had the water pulsed with sound like it did now. While running down the rapids, he had been dimly aware of a relentless series of hammer-blows coming from the mill at the far end of the pool. Now they reverberated loudly in his ears, coming at him from all directions through the water.

To conserve air, he allowed himself to be carried effortlessly along – his toes churning-up clouds of silt in his wake.

Forced back to the surface to breathe, he thrust himself off the muddy bottom with his hands and feet. As his head broke surface, he heard a yell from the shore. With only enough time for one quick gasp, he allowed himself to sink again – immediately swept along by the speeding under-current.

What had he just seen? Half a dozen men lined up along the right-hand bank, all raising bows in his direction. In front of him and slightly to his left, the water-wheel turning slowly – spray cascading from its descending blades. The Forester, clinging to the sluice-gate and staring up at a man who was creeping along the bank towards him. A man with a drawn-sword in his hand. A man who looked just like the assassin.

As the current strengthened, Jacob realised to his horror that he was about to be carried straight into the water-wheel. Although he had never steered a boat in his life, the instincts of his maritime forebears must have come into play. By pressing his broken sword slant-wise into the mud, he twisted his body in the Forester's direction. A sudden pressure of water along his left flank threatened to tear the sword from his grasp, but he held on to it doggedly. With the broken blade ploughing a ragged furrow in the silt, he kicked out with his legs to drive himself towards his master.

When the thrash of the mill wheel's descending blades warned him of their proximity, he risked raising his head above the water again. The assassin was now kneeling on the bank directly above the Forester – with his sword pointing downwards and ready to deliver the death-thrust.

The Forester had very little choice: either he could stay where he was and get skewered – or he could let go and be swept under the water wheel. Either way, he was a dead man.

So intent was the assassin on his murderous task that he didn't notice Jacob until it was too late. As he lunged downwards with his sword, the lad surged up out of the pool with his broken blade held above his head. Falling back, he slashed down at the assassin's wrist with all his might. It bit into flesh. Crimson blood spurted from severed veins. With a shriek of surprise and pain, the assassin dropped his sword. It fell into the pool – glinted once and then sank out of sight.

Attempting to staunch the flow of blood with his uninjured hand, the assassin lost his balance and plunged headfirst into the swirling water. Immediately, he was caught up in the current, swept round into the mill-race and sucked down beneath the thrashing blades. With a sickening SCRAUNCH, the wheel juddered to a standstill.

Everything went quiet. Even that incessant hammering had stopped.

"Thank God you came back, lad," gasped the Forester, struggling once again to haul himself up out of the water. "He would have done for me, and no mistake."

Jacob said nothing. He was too busy watching one of the assassin's accomplices, who was rummaging-about in a pouch which he had just picked-up from the grass.

"Tis no use," the man cried, tossing the bag aside. "There is no money here." Peering down at the fugitives who were still clinging to the side boards of the mill-race, he added:

"Yow might as well come up. We shall not hurt thee now, for there is no longer any profit in it."

By this time, the mill owner was hurrying out to see what had befallen his precious machinery. On hearing his approach, the cut-throats turned-about and squelched self-consciously off towards the road.

Now that the water wheel was jammed, its blades provided handy footholds for the pair to climb. But just as they were being escorted into the mill itself, they heard a sudden commotion on the distant road. Golden banners were waving, men were shouting and swords were flashing. Evidently, the Baron's soldiers had arrived and now they were engaging with the robbers.

The Forester grunted. "That is typical! They arrive too late to prevent an attack, but they are ready enough to take charge once the crisis is over." He stopped dead in his tracks – his expression, grim. "Or could it have been *planned* that way?"

CHAPTER FIFTEEN

The Steward of Dudley Castle marched briskly into its Great Hall and sprang onto a vacant bench. Sweeping his crimson cloak around him, he turned to face the soldiers who were seated around the walls and raised his arm to command their silence.

"MEN," he cried, "You may have heard that Lord Roger's killer is dead – thanks to young Jacques over there." He was pointing at Jacob, who was lounging between two men at arms and munching happily on one of his grandmother's pies. From time to time, he would toss a morsel of pastry to the garrison's mascot... a tame young jackdaw.

After waiting impatiently for the roar of approval to subside, the Steward continued:

"And now that we can *prove* that the Wyntertons were implicated, they will be brought to account at the next Court of Assize." Again, he waited for the sounds of approbation to die away. "And as for *thee,* young man…" Leaping lightly off the bench, he marched across to Jacob and encompassed his upper-arm with his powerful fingers. "I hear that you pack a hefty swing with this sword-arm of yours. Doubtless, all that practice with your wooden blade hath stood thee in good stead." He turned in search of the Forester, who was drawing himself a tankard of 'small-ale' from a freshly-supplied barrel. "See that this lad gets some proper training before we let him loose on any more of our enemies."

The Forester gritted his teeth but said nothing.

Flushing with embarrassment, Jacob stood up and bowed stiffly from the waist.

"Sire," he cried. "By your leave, I have changed my mind. Fighting is too bloody and dangerous for me! I should rather be a cookney and go back to helping my Gran in the bake-house."

"Going to stick to slicing apples, eh lad?" laughed the Steward, patting the lad on the back. "Well so be it."

As the crowded hall reverberated with the sounds of merriment, the Forester put aside his suspicions (for the time being) and hauled himself unsteadily to his feet.

"Here's to the lad who saved my life," he cried, turning to the crowd and raising his leather tankard above his head. "TO JACQUES."

"TCHAK!" squawked the jackdaw, flapping its clipped wings excitedly.

"I thank you," said the Forester, grinning down at the strutting bird. "'Jack' does seem to be a more fitting name for an Englishman." He raised his tankard once more.

"So HERE'S TO JACK O' THE BEANS! " he bellowed.

"TO JACK O' BEANS!" the assembled multitude cried, raising their jugs and tankards in salute.

Just outside the doorway, Jacob's grandmother flushed with pride. Perhaps he was not such a bad lad after all… whatever he chose to call himself.

THE END

Lightning Source UK Ltd.
Milton Keynes UK
UKOW02f0728140317
296533UK00001B/3/P